SLAVE TRADE

SLAVE TRADE

JUDGE, JURY, & EXECUTIONER™ BOOK FIVE

CRAIG MARTELLE

MICHAEL ANDERLE

DISRUPTIVE IMAGINATION

CONNECT WITH THE AUTHORS

Craig Martelle Social

Website & Newsletter:
http://www.craigmartelle.com

Facebook:
https://www.facebook.com/AuthorCraigMartelle/

Michael Anderle Social

Website: http://kurtherianbooks.com/

Email List: http://kurtherianbooks.com/email-list/
Facebook:
https://www.
facebook.com/TheKurtherianGambitBooks/

THE SLAVE TRADE TEAM

Thanks to our Beta Readers

Micky Cocker, James Caplan, Kelly O'Donnell, and John Ashmore

Thanks to the JIT Readers

Daniel Weigert
James Caplan
Diane L. Smith
Larry Omans
Nicole Emens
Jeff Eaton
John Ashmore
Kelly O'Donnell
Misty Roa
Micky Cocker
Dorothy Lloyd
Paul Westman

If I've missed anyone, please let me know!

Editor
Lynne Stiegler

We can't write without those who support us
On the home front, we thank you for being there for us

We wouldn't be able to do this for a living if it weren't for our
readers
We thank you for reading our books

CHAPTER ONE

Corran, Slave Pits

"Go fuck yourself!" She spat blood for emphasis. The Corranite threw his head back and laughed. When he finished, he fixed her with an intense glare. The captive was still furious. He turned, swinging one last time, knowing that it would do the trick.

The sickening crunch was followed by the sound of a body hitting the deck. He glanced down to ensure she was unconscious.

"When you wake up, we'll talk again," the fibrous alien promised. "Or *I'll* talk and you'll get sold, which is how it's going to end up, no matter what." He spat a yellow glob on her leg. "That's a reminder to remember your place."

Federation Border Station 7

Vered fired the railgun at the target bounding back and forth at the edge of his vision. Lindy fired and laughed as the disc disintegrated when her stream of hypervelocity projectiles ripped through it.

"I used to be better at this," Red groused through a half-smile.

"If you're letting me win, I'll kick your ass upside-down and sideways." She kept her railgun pointed into space while standing with a fist pressed to her hip.

"Did I let you hit your targets? Is that some mind trick that I'm unaware of? If so, I need to do more of it to keep the foreplay talk coming." He winked at her.

She kicked at him, but he easily dodged the half-hearted attempt. "I may just kick your ass for the greater good of the whole galaxy."

With a nod, they agreed to stow their weapons and call it a day. The hangar bay was empty at that time of morning. *Peacekeeper* was anchored to the deck behind them, and a forcefield across the broad opening that led to space kept the atmosphere in. Their target practice had used the emptiness as their backstop. The railgun projectiles would eventually stop moving. Until then, there was a designated no-fly zone in a cone away from the station.

It was nice to know lawyers who could do the paperwork to jump through those bureaucratic hoops.

Until Rivka presented Red with the bill for the no-fly-zone marker buoys. He almost had to sell his yacht to pay for them, but Ankh arranged a loan.

"It chaps my ass that I owe him credits," Red complained.

"Why? We get to keep the yacht, even though most of our pay goes to its required maintenance and upkeep. Maybe you should rent it to people? I heard the Magistrate talk about some of her investments. Let your money make money, and if you don't have money, let your property earn money while you're not using it."

"Then I could pay off our little friend that much sooner." Red rubbed his face, and Lindy wrapped an arm around his waist.

"What would you do without me?

"Be bored. Lonely. Probably beg the Magistrate for more dangerous missions. Beat the shit out of bad guys. Yeah—that one. Beating the shit out of bad buys is a favorite way to expend excess energy in an otherwise meaningless existence."

The smirk on Lindy's face suggested she didn't agree. She stopped as their datapads vibrated at the same time.

"Saved by the bell," Red mumbled.

"Saved by the Magistrate's impeccable timing, more like." They scanned the message.

All hands are recalled. We're leaving on our next case as soon as I get back to the ship.

"Do we have time for pizza?" Red asked, waggling his eyebrows at Lindy.

"*That's* the first thing you think of? What's the case?" Lindy wondered, watching Red tap furiously on his datapad. "I'm worried. Usually the magistrate explains more. Calls a meeting. We all chat, then we go. Something has her spooked. Plus, we've only been back for four days. We were supposed to get three weeks off. Are you listening to me?"

"The Magistrate can have some, too. I ordered one of those gross Moonstokle things for her. We better hurry to the ship," Red said. Lindy rotated at the waist and drove her fist into his chest. It thudded against something hard.

CRAIG MARTELLE & MICHAEL ANDERLE

She yowled in pain. "What the hell do you have in your vest?"

"What the hell are you punching me for?" Red shot back, screwing up his face at her pain and anger. "Dammit. I'm sorry." He dropped to a knee to get a better look at her hand.

He grimaced, but quickly tried to cover it with a smile.

"It's not as broken as it could be." He sounded as hopeful and upbeat as he could.

"At least it's throbbing less." Lindy tucked her injured hand against her stomach, and with her good hand, tapped Red's chest, undid the pouch, and pulled out a spare magazine for the railgun. "You brought extra ammo? Planning on missing a lot of the targets?"

"It's contingency stuff. The Magistrate keeps me on my toes. I can't risk failing her, which means everywhere I go, I have my gear. At least, most of it."

Lindy turned to the ship. They hadn't been more than fifty meters from it. There would have been time to return for any equipment they needed. At least that's what she had thought. "You don't think we would have had time to go to the ship?"

"No," Red replied simply. "Just like the Magistrate doesn't hesitate when it's time to deliver Justice, I can't hesitate when it's time to protect her. I can't leave her ass hanging out in the wind, and I won't leave yours either. If someone came through that door," Red pointed at the far wall, "they could cut me off from the ship, but I'd still be able to fight from cover there and over there until I could get to them and finish them."

Lindy nodded slowly. "I'm sorry I let you down."

"How so?

"By not being as ready as you."

Red threw his head back and laughed. "I was ready for both of us. I have two spare magazines and extra water. Even an extra food bar."

She pulled his face to hers for a fierce kiss before whispering, "I'm still mad at you."

"What did I do now?"

"You weren't listening to me, and then you changed the subject!"

"Magistrate explains, we chat, but this time we're rushing off without knowing. I heard you just fine, but it's all speculation, and I don't like to speculate. How about we return to the ship, clean our weapons, and ask her when she arrives?"

"I'm still mad at you!"

All hands are recalled. We're leaving on our next case as soon as I get back to the ship.

Rivka watched the message go. She wasn't sure how much longer the prep work with Grainger would take, but she knew they'd be leaving soon. The initial case brief had her blood boiling.

Grainger and Rivka were side by side in the Magistrates' conference room. Together they glared at the images on the screen.

"Slavery is legal on Corran," Rivka spat, distaste permeating her words. Her face contorted as she spoke. "How is that possible? This is the Federation!"

CRAIG MARTELLE & MICHAEL ANDERLE

"Corran isn't in the Federation. *Yet*, that is. We're close to bringing them on board, but until then, they can conduct business as they wish, since they're still an independent planet. But," he paused for effect and raised one finger, "they *are* on the border of Federation territory, and no one can transit Federation space with slaves."

"Then how in the holy fuck are they still in business?"

"Slavers. The worst humanity has to offer is nothing compared to the Corranites. You need to find and cut their supply chain. Catch every Federation citizen involved and charge them. Justice needs to come swift and heavy."

Rivka spoke through clenched teeth. "And if I have to knock a few Corranite heads?"

"Please don't." Grainger looked at his lap. "They have something or other that is necessary for both the miniaturized power supplies and the small Gate engines. The Federation is keen on sealing a long-term deal. You have to walk on eggshells where the Corranites are concerned."

"After you said they were worse than any human slaver, you tell me to play nice with them? My fist is going to land squarely in their slaver faces if they don't tread lightly around me!" Rivka declared. She stood and started to pace. "I have to turn a blind eye to the injustice in front of me to find the injustice behind me? Jurisdictional issues. What does a visa and access to Corran grant? She tapped her datapad. "Chaz, start taking notes, please."

She walked back and forth but didn't say anything further. Her forehead wrinkled with dismay, creating a single brow above a dark scowl. Grainger crossed his arms and leaned back in his chair, tilting his head one way and then the other as if the changed angles would show him a different side of Magistrate Rivka Anoa.

"Corran law and protections of non-citizens. Everything the Federation has in regards to human and alien trafficking. Kidnapping and detention of sentient species. Cross-border transfers as they relate to Federation space." Rivka recited the areas of law she wanted Chaz to research. "Is this shithole in the Corrhen Cluster?"

"How did you guess?" Grainger asked, his voice neutral because it wasn't a surprise that she had guessed.

"Fucking Morinvaille was as much of the cluster as I wanted to see. What is the continued influence of the Mandolin Partnership out there? If I remember correctly, at least one ship of the pirate fleet escaped. I'm sure we'll find that bastard again."

"Maybe they've discovered the error of their ways, and now they're plying the trade routes as mobile pet washers?"

Rivka nodded for a moment, but stopped and glared at Grainger.

"What are the chances of that?"

"Pet washing? Fairly low, I suspect."

She groaned and clenched her hands into fists before continuing. "There's no way they aren't doing their thing. Their fleet will have grown, but not by much. We'll have to deal with maybe three or four ships."

"On a serious side note, you'll need to get approval before asking the Bad Company for help. General Reynolds and Nathan Lowell need to be on the same page before Terry Henry Walton's force can be brought to bear."

Rivka crossed her arms and tipped her head back to

examine the senior Magistrate. "Have you become a bureaucrat, Leibchen?"

"I have no ass left because I allowed the redeployment of strategic assets. The Bad Company's budget is tied to paying gigs. They aren't covered out of Federation funds. They are also expensive, orders of magnitude higher than what we spend, and they aren't a Federation asset as far as the common woman knows. Therefore, we can't pay for them unless there is a compelling need. And next time, it won't be just my ass that they chew up and hand back to me, it'll be my head. You know where shit rolls."

"Downhill. Right to me. But it was a massive failure on the Federation's part to allow things to get so bad that one little trigger sent an entire planet over the brink into civil war. I don't buy it."

Grainger started to laugh and leaned forward to hunch over the conference table. "We'll all be buying it," he finally managed to say. "We can get their approval in short order, or at least approval for some kind of asset. Your corvette is tough, but it's not made to go up against a major warship of any sort. With the recruitment of the Harborians and their poor performance against the destroyer, they need more active deployments to earn their chops. *War Axe* is off the table unless Lance Reynolds and Nathan Lowell jointly approve."

"Even if Terry's wombat is with us?"

"That's a completely different issue. He wants to come for a visit... Hey, are you trying to find a loophole in your instructions?"

"I *am* a lawyer..." Rivka started, but stopped when Grainger raised a hand.

"You know the intent of your guidance. Don't make me take your ship and Red's yacht away and sell them to pay your debt to the Bad Company. If they aren't somewhere else doing their job, they're not getting paid. And don't blame them. You know Terry and Char would do anything for one of the good guys, and for some unholy reason, they've awarded you that title. Don't fucking do it."

Rivka flopped into the chair opposite Grainger. "This one already has me twisted into a knot. My first instinct is that the entire planet of Corran needs to be purged by fire."

"It's because you care, Rivka. Because you can't stand to see the injustices of the universe put on display because one planet believes it's okay to trade in sentient creatures. If you lose your ability to look at these things dispassionately, you become both ineffective and a loose cannon. We can't have either of those. You will be the best of us, and someday you'll be sitting in this chair talking to other Magistrates about how to enforce the law, how to deliver Justice, and how to do it without losing yourself in the process." He fixed her with his clear blue eyes. "You call me if you start going off the rails. Beau is in touch with Chaz, so I should have a heads-up, but don't lose it out there. Your crew is counting on you. *I'm* counting on you, which means the entire Federation legal system needs you to do the right thing from a sound foundation based in the law. If you could do that while taking out Mackestray and K'Twillis, then you can do that anywhere."

"Those guys left a huge trail of breadcrumbs."

"As will the slavers. Some are legitimate, as horrible as that sounds. Leave those alone, but the ones that aren't? They need to be brought up to speed right damn now."

"The illegitimate slavers will suffer mightily and will be the case law for future transgressors. I know Bethany Anne set the precedent with her anti-slaving stance, but Federation law isn't cut and dried that it's a capital crime. I want it to be punishable by death."

Grainger stood and put on his Magistrates' jacket, then nodded and turned to the door. He stopped to say something quietly over his shoulder. "I've heard that depriving someone of their life, even if they aren't dead, can be equated to capital murder." He opened the door and walked out.

Rivka accessed her datapad and tapped briefly. *I'm on my way.* She sent the message and stuffed the pad into the inside pocket of her jacket, then adjusted the Magistrate pin on her collar and headed out.

CHAPTER TWO

Rivka stalked across the hangar deck, passing the All Guns Blazing delivery guy on his way out. She started to shake her head. Before reaching the ship, she saw Red waving at her from the open hatch.

"All present and accounted for, Magistrate," he declared.

"Don't tell me you ordered food." She hurried up the ramp, and once inside, mashed the big red button to seal the ship.

"Okay. I won't tell you." Red shrugged and lumbered down the short passageway, turned at the open hatch to the bridge, and entered the ship's main space. It was a combination of recreation room, workout room, meeting room, and dining area. "Can't go on a mission with an empty stomach, Magistrate."

The smell of pizza reminded her how hungry she was even though she didn't think it had been that long since she last ate.

Red pointed at one of the boxes.

"Moonstokle?"

"Yes. I refuse to touch it," he said, making a show of pulling two boxes out from underneath the Magistrate's pie.

Jay strolled in, still in her pajamas. She yawned, unable to cover her mouth since her arms were filled with wombat.

Yeah, Floyd cheered when she saw that everyone was back. Lindy scratched behind her ears, and Rivka stopped reaching for a slice and paid attention to Floyd for a few moments.

"What's everyone doing?"

"We're getting ready to fly. Judging by the Magistrate's expression, there are asses somewhere that need kicking." Red stuffed an entire slice into his mouth so he wouldn't be asked to explain further. Lindy helped herself, elbowing Red out of the way.

"I love pizza for breakfast." Jay set Floyd on the deck and worked her way into the fray. "What time is it?"

"Chaz, can you ask Ankh to come out here, please?" Rivka interrupted. She turned to Jay. "It's lunchtime."

Ankh's door flew open and he stormed out, as much as a meter-tall alien with an oversized head could storm.

"I don't have time for this," he declared, crossing his arms and glaring up at Rivka.

"I respect your time, Ankh. I'll make this quick." She put her slice down, picking off two pieces of the alien version of pineapple and eating them. "There are slave traders operating on the planet Corran in the Corrhen Cluster. Slaving is legal on Corran since they aren't a Federation signatory, but there's a lot of illegal trading going on by persons who are subject to Federation laws. We're going to find those who are selling people, and we're going to stop them."

Lindy stopped chewing and stared at the mural on the bulkhead. There was a section with a sun shining on a verdant planet with people enjoying themselves. Five, plus a cat and a wombat. Red ate another slice, but without the show this time. Jay stopped mid-reach.

"There are people who sell other people?"

"There are races where it's okay to do that, but Corran is close to joining the Federation. Maybe we'll get lucky and *help* them close down their meat markets."

Ankh started tapping his foot, and Rivka stared at it until he stopped.

"I hear they have Crenellian slaves," Rivka taunted.

"We make lousy slaves," he replied. "But I agree that this practice needs to end. Let Erasmus and me know when we're close. I assume you don't have a plan?"

Rivka's mouth opened and closed and she stammered, but they weren't words.

"The usual." Ankh returned to his room and closed the door.

"It chaps my ass that I owe him money," Red whispered to Lindy. "But he's not wrong."

Rivka stepped forward until she was chest to chest with Vered. Carefully he reached around her and snagged another slice of pizza. He took a slow bite, his eyes fixed on hers.

"Are we that bad?" Rivka finally asked. "Don't answer that. We always have a loose plan that gets refined as we gather more information and build our case. And then we formulate a clear take-down strategy on the perps before delivering Justice."

"That's how I see it," Red said through a mouthful of hot pizza. "You left out the explosions, the blood, and the running, but everything else is right."

Jay recovered sufficiently to share a slice with Floyd. Rivka turned to Lindy, looking for support.

Lindy obliged her. "Your job cannot be relegated to a diagram of steps from start to finish. You deal with more unknowns than an engineer like Ankh. He can't write a program without knowing the steps it must follow. He cannot address variables if he doesn't know their parameters. I think we have a challenging job, but you give us the best chance of success. I haven't been on all the missions, but Red and Jay have. You've never failed, Magistrate. That's the team I like being on."

"I agree," Jay mumbled, swallowing before she continued. "It's like my old home. Say we arrive on a space station and don't know where to go for a meal. We ask around until we find a restaurant, but they don't serve anything good. We find a different restaurant, but they serve spoiled food. The Magistrate shuts them down, but we keep going because we're still hungry. We haven't achieved what we went there for. We find someone getting mugged, and of course, we stop that. Then we finally find the good restaurant, but they're closed until dinner, so we have to cool our heels—and we're not good at waiting."

"So we break in and make our own dinner," Red finished for her.

"We don't break in," Rivka corrected. Red raised one eyebrow. "Often."

"Slave trade. Sounds like I'm going to need a shower after just talking about it." Lindy's lip curled.

The ship lifted off and carefully maneuvered into open space. "Magistrate, may I have the coordinates where we're going?" Chaz asked.

"Back to the Corrhen Cluster, Chaz. Planet Corran."

"Do you want to arrive close to the planet?"

"I don't think so. Let's shoot for the edge of the heliosphere and get the lay of the land. I need to do a great deal of research before we storm the castle walls.

"We'll Gate momentarily to the edge of the heliosphere. No one will know we've arrived until you want to make your presence known."

"I like the way you think, Chaz. Consolidate the information I asked you to pull and prepare to Gate on my order."

"Standing by, Magistrate."

I help! Floyd cried, scratching at the table.

"Why are you so upset, little girl?" Jay wondered, stroking the wombat's fur to calm her.

My friends are angry and sad, Floyd explained.

"Just for now, Floyd," Red said as he continued to eat. Lindy closed the lid on the second box to cut him off. He smirked at her. "We're going to save a lot of people from the fate of being owned by someone else."

It's all I know, Floyd said slowly.

Jay hugged the furry beast. "You're free, Floyd."

I'm loved, the wombat corrected. *I can't be free. I would die. I grew up with slaves on a planet far away. Terry saved me. Saved all of us.*

"Yes, he did," Rivka agreed. "You're our friend, Floyd. If

you need anything, we will move mountains to make sure you get it."

"Unless you keep eating my pizza," Red grumbled.

"Give her your fucking pizza, you monster!" Rivka pounded the table for emphasis. Without hesitation, Red put the slice in front of Floyd's face. She took it gently before gobbling it down.

"Maybe you should give her yours. It's not fit to eat," Red said softly without looking at the Magistrate.

Rivka started to laugh. "At least we know you have a soul."

"I know. I'm a big softie. *Slavers*. I need to keep up my strength. If I know anything about Magistrate Rivka Anoa and her missions, the bad guys are going to be begging for buttermilk before this is all over."

Rivka pointed at Red and then Lindy. "Did you guys get married?"

Red coughed until Lindy pounded on his back.

"What makes you say that?"

"You act like you're married. You know, you're doing all the talking, and Lindy can't get a word in edgewise."

Red turned to Lindy, and she nodded.

"So you *are* married?" Rivka clarified.

"No," Lindy replied when Red threw his hands up in surrender. "We have reservations for next week, so if we don't make it back, the station administrator will scratch us off the list. We'll just keep the honeymoon going for that much longer."

"That's my girl," Red said proudly.

She stabbed a finger into his chest. "That's my big husky hunk of man candy."

"You two were made for each other," Rivka mumbled as she grabbed two slices and headed for the bridge. "Chaz! We got work to do."

We got work to do! Floyd cried happily.

"Yes, we do, little girl. We'll see if you can come, but if you can't, don't be sad. We're making the universe a safer place for people like you," Jay explained.

Hamlet picked that moment to make his appearance. He vaulted onto the table where the food was, draping himself across the middle and grooming his face.

"Get down!" Red reached down to swat the cat, earning himself a long streak of parallel scratches. "Who put the cat in the Pod-doc?"

"Maybe he's naturally faster than you?" Jay asked. She reached up and scratched his chin and he stretched lazily, exposing his soft belly fur. She scratched him quickly until he curled around her hand and tried to bite a finger. She pulled her hand away so quickly that his jaws snapped shut on air, his claws exposed on all four paws.

"Amazeballs," Red remarked. Lindy looked at the empty place where Jay's hand used to be. Hamlet started licking himself as if nothing had happened.

The Corranite reached through the bars and yanked the human woman to her feet. The bruise on her cheek extended to her now swollen-shut eye. He wasn't pleased. She blinked at him with her good eye and ripped at his arm with her bare hands.

"You'll go for a good price as soon as your face returns

to normal." He grunted and pulled her head closer to his. She snorted and spat, and the Corranite laughed heartily. "Is that all you have?"

Her look of triumph turned to fear as he called on every fiber of his being to bring up a great ball of phlegm. She fought against his grip, but he was too strong. When he unloaded on her, it was like getting hit in the face by an egg from a fifty-kilo Grasshawk. She gagged and puked.

Yellow bile dripped from her lips, a testament to the time that had passed since she'd last eaten. She scrubbed the disgusting stuff from her face and flung it on his leg.

"I'm going to get a rag and ice. You're going to clean up and then put ice on that bruise. Next time, I may not be so kind." He released her head and pushed her away, not hard enough to knock her down but hard enough to remind her who was in charge.

She glared at him from one eye. He walked away without further posturing.

The woman sighed heavily once he was gone and scrubbed at her face to remove his filth. *Ice to draw a higher price?* She didn't think so. "Seequa, what have you gotten yourself into?" the woman asked.

An exclusive party with rich guys, but she was with her friends.

Her so-called friends. None of *them* seemed to be in the cages. She remembered dancing under a rainbow strobe, and the next thing she knew, she woke up in a slave pen.

"I didn't do a damn thing. Those fuckers can stand the fuck by. I'm getting out of here, and then I'm coming for them. Kidnap *me*, will you! FUCK ALL Y'ALL!" she bellowed. "Ice my eye? How about you don't hit me, motherfucker?"

Her knuckles turned white as she clenched her fists in anticipation of the Corranite's return.

Peacekeeper sat serenely at the heliosphere's edge, little more than a hole in space. Corran was three planets away, second from the system's star. Three tiny moons orbited in fast ellipses, their pull on the planet's surface minimal. Traffic control worked around the moons to keep unsuspecting ships from powering down at a geosynchronous location, only to find themselves in the path of a mindless and merciless chunk of rock. Orbits well beyond the planet's gravity were safe, and it required the utmost coordination to keep ships from competing with each other for the few open flight windows.

There seemed to be more ships than opportunities to reach the planet's surface. Flight control struggled to maintain order.

"That's a real shit show down there," Red offered. Chaz was piping the feed to the rec room as well as the bridge.

Rivka half-listened. She was neck-deep in reading legal treatises, and her eyes were bloodshot from perusing the mountain of words.

"How do you think we'll get to the planet?" Lindy asked.

"Hitch a ride?" Red put one finger on the back of his hand as he made it fly through the air and land on the table. "Wouldn't be the first time."

"We might get shot for pulling rank to get a slot in an open window."

"We might get shot anyway. Our luck isn't good when it comes to not getting shot at."

"Maybe it's a gift?" Lindy smiled and tilted her head. Red stared. "What?"

"Sometimes I need to remind myself not to take my best friend for granted. I look at every mission..."

"Case!" Rivka yelled through the bridge's open hatch.

"...as if we're going into combat. Even on the station, I can't relax and think of a time when people won't shoot at the Magistrate. They're afraid of her, as well they should be. And I think of my partner and how we can tactically deploy to do our jobs, but I also feel compelled to protect you. I know that's not what you want or need, and I love not having to worry about that. I also love that you have my back. And what started this whole thing was, I love seeing you smile."

"My shmoopie bodyguard!" Rivka shouted.

Red scowled. Lindy smiled, showing the tip of her tongue between her teeth. He relented and smiled back.

"I'm in the right place doing what I was meant to do. We're going to locate some slavers, and then we're going to ruin their day. Hopefully, they will give us a good reason and the Magistrate leaves something for us." Lindy hesitated, and her eyes started to glisten. She blinked quickly. "I love you, Vered."

"It's a shmoopfest!" Rivka was standing in the hatch and slowly clapping.

"What the hell? Don't you have homework or something?" Red was torn between looking at Rivka and trying to make time with his partner.

"I'm done with what I need to do. We need to talk about how we're going to peel this onion. Can you get Ankh, please?"

Red ran a hand down Lindy's arm and it somehow found its way to her backside, which he cupped appreciatively.

"Our wedding vows should probably include 'I promise to grab your butt every day,' because it's going to happen, isn't it?"

"Probably," Red said before letting go and taking the few steps to the stateroom that Ankh had designated as his workshop. "Come on, big man. Team meeting."

Ankh strolled out, holding his hands over his ears. His night-vision goggles had become a permanent fixture on his forehead, and they faced Red like an extra set of eyes. "Next time warn me before you show up at my door and do your impression of a dying bistok."

Red cupped his hands around his mouth and started bellowing, and Lindy jabbed him in the ribs. "What the god-awful noise is that?"

"A dying bistok?" Red looked for support from the crew. Only contorted faces looked back at him.

"I hope I never hear that sound again," Jay stated.

"Seconded," Rivka declared.

"Fine." Red worked his way into the small kitchen area, tapped the food processor screen, and waited until a bar popped out.

"Didn't you just eat?" Lindy asked.

"That was a couple hundred light years ago," Red replied before taking a bite.

"Point to Red." Rivka motioned with one finger in the air, marking a single digit in her bodyguard's favor. Her face turned solemn as she started to brief her team. "The slave trade is highly regulated on Corran. Each sentient being who is to be sold has to undergo medical and psychological evaluations. To the untrained eye, it appears to be a cooperative and mutually beneficial system."

"Unless you're the slave," Jay said softly.

"Exactly. They rarely disqualify a being from the auction block, but when it happens, they simply go to a different block and are sold as defective merchandise. So, no change for the victims. We are here to find those who are bringing illegal captives to Corran. Once they are introduced into the system, our access to information becomes nonexistent. Corran is not a Federation signatory. They don't even owe us the courtesy of allowing us to land, but Reynolds is in negotiations for them to accommodate this request. They know that if they join the Federation, their slave trade will instantly become illegal. There can be no casual phaseout of such a practice."

"Accessing their systems will not be a problem," Ankh said in his small voice. "How far are we willing to push?"

"Not being seen is better than pulling every byte from their storage systems. They cannot know it was us digging behind the curtain."

"So we can't push too hard, but I expect to find every byte and bit of data you need without leaving a trace. I can do it from here. I prefer not to leave the ship."

"We'll drop your devices wherever you need us to," Red

said, giving the Crenellian a thumbs-up. Ankh's face remained unreadable as he looked up at the oversized human.

"You keep Floyd company!" Jay minced no words. Ankh turned his head and glanced at her but didn't say anything. The wombat tottered to him and nuzzled his arm. Jay pointed at him. "Pet her."

Ankh mechanically stroked the fur on her head.

"Don't you feel better and happier?" Jay asked with a smile.

"No," Ankh replied simply, but he didn't stop petting Floyd.

"We will go to the main slave market, and from there, work our way up until we meet with the governor-general." Rivka noted the distaste on the faces of her team. "It's as fun as watching child porn to build a case against a scumbag."

"Have you had to do that?" Lindy wondered.

"Thank the gods, no, but it wouldn't get that far. I'd look into his mind and know in an instant which way he needed to die."

"I think you're serious," Red said. Rivka raised one eyebrow. "You're going to see some horrible shit from these people. How can we help keep you sane?"

"That could be the best question you've ever asked, Red. How indeed? I think the best thing is to not touch anyone who might not be involved in the illegal stuff, so the initial plan is to not touch *anyone* with my bare hands. Run blocker for me so no one gets too close."

"Done," Red and Lindy declared together.

"Jay. I need you to stay strong. This is the twilight of the slave trade. If Lance Reynolds is successful at bringing this planet into the Federation, the very last of the legal slave planets will be gone. We will break out the brooms and sweep the bad guys into the dustbins of history. We know there will be some who think themselves superior and won't let go. We'll fix them when the time is right, but for now, non-Corranites can get licensed to transport captured sentient cargo. With a license, they are protected inside this system. Regardless, some species are illegal to be slaves. Yollins are on that list, and so are humans. If we find one of those, we can request an immediate release."

"I sense a 'but' coming," Red interrupted.

"But," Rivka continued, "we have to get the release before we can detain the slaver and free the victim."

"Does that go for anyone who deserves to be freed?"

"They *all* deserve to be set free, but no. Only those on the sanctioned list are eligible to get a release."

Ankh, Lindy, Red, and Jay shared looks. Ankh closed his eyes, and three datapads buzzed.

"You guys aren't betting again, are you?" Rivka asked.

CHAPTER THREE

"We have been granted a priority clearance," Chaz relayed. The ship maneuvered between heavy haulers, freighters, yachts, and passenger ships.

"You're going to get us killed, Chaz!" Red exclaimed.

"Why don't you hail one of the freighters that's only carrying cargo? We can piggyback and move them to the front of the line. Then we'll have one friend, at least."

"Traffic Control has not approved that plan," the ship's AI warned.

"We'll squawk our beacon. They won't know the difference." Rivka shrugged.

"They won't know the difference between a corvette and a freighter ripping through their atmosphere?" Chaz grumbled.

"Was he nicer when he was less evolved?" Jay asked.

"Much nicer," Lindy replied.

"The *Tombo Queen* is pleased with your proposal and accepts your offer. They are moving out of line to meet us."

A massive ship lumbered through space. A yacht tried

to hold its ground, but soon realized that the freighter was coming regardless of their presence. They darted aside at the last instant, clearing the way for the *Queen*. Chaz expertly maneuvered *Peacekeeper* to roll in on top of the larger ship, then set it down and engaged the clamps.

"We're along for the ride," Chaz told them.

"Thank you. When we hit the ground, we'll need you two in full gear. Jay and I will wear body armor, but we won't be armed."

Red handed the Magistrate the neutron pulse weapon affectionately known as "Reaper." "You mean you won't *appear* to be armed."

"Sometimes there are such subtle nuances in the law," Rivka said. "And other times, there's brute force. I don't have the immunity here that I do on a Federation planet, but as long as the negotiations with Reynolds are ongoing, I have some protection. Make sure I don't need it."

"You're talking to yourself, right?" Red asked. "You know me: seen but not heard."

"I do, Red. And you're right, I'm talking to myself more than you guys." She looked at Jay, who put on her innocent face.

"It might be better if we don't visit the slave pens," Jay suggested meekly, looking down at the floor.

"It might, but I don't think that's in the cards. We're going to cut off their supply by taking out their legs. Reynolds is going to seal the deal and cut off their heads. There won't be anything left when we're done."

"And if Reynolds *doesn't* seal the deal?" Red knew the answer before he asked the question.

"Then we'll need to get the hell out of town right quick."

Red turned to Lindy. "We need to have an egress plan in mind at all times, so use our internal comm to keep it up to the minute. And Jay, please don't get adventurous. We will probably need you to make sure the way ahead is clear if we have to run for it. Ankh? You know we'll be contacting you and asking for something bizarre, like hacking an auto-barista to hook us up with mochaccinos."

"What's a mochaccino?" Ankh deadpanned.

"Exactly. That's why we need the system to flex to your indomitable will."

"You're not getting one," Ankh replied.

"Seats, please," Chaz requested. "We'll be entering Corran's atmosphere momentarily."

Rivka returned to the bridge, Ankh disappeared into his workshop again, and the others took seats in the rec room. Jay held Floyd in her arms and cooed into the wombat's ear. She giggled as the turbulence started.

Hamlet strolled out, getting tossed back and forth. He spread his legs wide and tried to balance. Lindy held out her arms and called to him. He worked his way close and she picked him up, holding the cat and petting him as the ship bounced and jerked.

Rivka watched the view outside the ship as shown on the main screen. "What does ground transport look like?"

"Most people in the city of Amberly use public transportation: high-speed monorails, people-movers, conveyors, and the like. Only executives and freight move on the limited streets. I have secured an automated aerovan, which should limit the delays."

"No drivers? Everything is automated?"

"Yes. The Corranites maintain strict control over all movement in the city. Facial recognition secures every door, every vehicle, and every room. You will have to register when you first board the aerovan, and then you'll be logged into their system."

"And all of that security is paid for by sentient trafficking." Rivka blew out a heavy breath.

"Very few slaves are mistreated, Magistrate and many, when given the choice of freedom, choose to continue their lives of servitude. Many begin their lives as servants under contract."

"Freedom means choosing what you want and living with the consequences of your decisions. Maybe those people were really given no choice, since the consequences of the alternative were too dire. Maybe their spirits were broken. Who knows the reason?

"For right now, none of that matters. Sentient Trafficking is covered under Federation Law, Title 4, Section 1, Physical Crimes Against the Individual. We can find predecessor crimes in the act of securing the being, such as assault and battery, kidnapping, theft by deception, and others. Within the statute, we have the Sentient Trafficking sub-section, which relates to moving illegally detained persons. Illegal Detention can be added if other elements are proven. And none of that applies to the Corranites. For them to be complicit, they have to be operating without a license or trading uncleared persons, but those can be remedied post facto, as in buying a license or having a doc look at the person and medically clear them to be sold. We need the Corranites to lead us to their suppliers."

"We could look at the ship below us," Chaz added.

"Don't tell me. You knew I didn't want to help a slaver!" Rivka raged.

"They had the four bodies hidden within their manifest. They are a cargo hauler first and foremost. This was a last-minute add, but I am very sorry that I missed it on my first pass, Magistrate."

"Ankh! Get into that ship and find out everything there is to know about the four slaves they're carrying." Rivka held tightly to the captain's chair until *Peacekeeper* broke through the upper atmosphere. As soon as the turbulence cleared, she bolted from her seat and ran to the back of the ship. "Chaz, no one gets off the *Queen* until I say so."

Rivka and her team huddled on the bridge. The freighter had landed, and they were awaiting clearance by Amberly Ground Control before departing. *Tombo Queen* wasn't answering her hails, but with Ankh's assistance, she suspected they'd be picking up soon.

Rivka started to tap her foot. As she turned to Ankh, the screen came to life. "*Peacekeeper*, this is *Tombo Queen*. How can we assist you?"

"Thank you for taking my call," Rivka replied, using the old timers' vernacular. "I'm Magistrate Rivka Anoa, and it's been brought to my attention that you have illegally transported four sentient beings through Federation space for the purpose of selling them. Under my authority as Magistrate, I am seizing your vessel, your cargo, and your crew.

You will remain locked down and on the ground until I have time to deal with you."

"Wait, wait!" the nasal voice pleaded. "We don't have any sentient species aboard."

"Yourself included?" Rivka shot back. "You will stand by as I open the doors between their cell and the outer hatch. When they appear, I'll ask them about it."

"Wait! My first officer has just informed me that there was a last-minute add to the manifest. I am appalled that my vessel, which has a perfect record, would be so sullied. I shall execute him immediately."

"You'll do no such thing, unless you want me to bring you up on murder charges in addition to *all* the other charges you've racked up?"

"How were you able to secure our doors?" the captain asked,

"That's probably a question your sentient cargo is asking. Here's what you need to do: roll out the red carpet for your guests, Explain the misunderstanding. Treat them like royalty. And give them all your credits. Your ship and cargo are still impounded, and you, sir, are now a convicted felon. When I have the time to deal with you, I'll look at your case from an appellate viewpoint."

Sounds of a struggle came over the connection, and they ended with a thud and the thump of a body hitting the floor. "This is the first officer. I have taken the captain into custody and will secure him until your arrival. Your orders will be fully complied with."

The line went dead.

"You didn't have to see into anyone's mind or punch anyone in their ugly face," Red remarked.

"The day is looking up, my friends!" Rivka declared, and they headed for the hatch. "Chaz, detach us and find us a nice parking spot."

Peacekeeper's clamps released with an audible clang and the ship's thrusters lifted it gently, slipped sideways, and settled to the tarmac. Red was up front, hand hovering over the big red button. Jay was behind him, and Lindy waited for the Magistrate so the bodyguard could bring up the rear. She and Red were fully armed and armored, included helmets and face shields.

"Do it," Rivka ordered, and Red mashed the button. The door opened to a waning sun that still put out plenty of warmth. The planet was huge, much bigger than the norm, and the gravity was already weighing on them. The habitable areas of the planet were relatively small. More planet, less space. Fewer natural inhabitants.

"Maybe that's how they justify the slave trade," Rivka said aloud, making her way into the open air. It was clean and fresh, and they all breathed deeply.

Red moved down the ramp, looking for threats as he always did. The barrel of his railgun swung with his eyes. Red noted the individual at the bottom of the stairs and discounted him as a threat, but he blocked the male's view of Rivka. Geared up, Red cut an imposing figure.

"Who are you?" Red asked before the individual could speak.

"I am Palatius Lore, representative of the governor-general. He will be pleased to host you at his official residence. Please follow me."

Red stepped aside at the bottom of the ramp.

"I'm Magistrate Rivka Anoa. I was looking to visit the market first."

"That's out of the question," Palatius replied simply. "We are going to see the governor-general before anything else."

"Are you so used to taking people's free will that you would do it to a Federation Magistrate?" Jayita asked. Rivka raised her hand to stop her, but it was too late.

"You can always leave," he said, motioning for them to go back up the ramp.

"My apologies, Mister Lore. We would be more than happy to accept the governor-general's hospitality. Please lead on."

We used to have a plan, Red said softly over the internal comm. *This is the second quickest... No, make that the third quickest that our original plan has gone out the airlock.*

Nobody give this knothead or the governor-general grief, please, Rivka fixed Jay with an unblinking glare. Jay tried to smile, but it fell flat. Red and Lindy were doing their respective guard things and didn't respond.

"Can you tell us about Amberly during our drive? It's my first time here, and I have to compliment you on how lovely your city is!"

"You have to compliment me? Were you expecting a trash heap? And I had nothing to do with how this city looks. The wisdom and artistry of those who built it are to be complimented." He shook his head and threw his fibrous hands down. "Federation arrogance grows old."

Douchebag, Red said over the internal comm.

Rivka smiled pleasantly, breathing Amberly's clean air

slowly and looking around as if she were on a stroll through a garden. "No matter. I'll enjoy it at my leisure."

She studied their host, a creature who appeared to be made of coiled fibers, like a tightly woven rug. He didn't appear to have skin, and it was disconcerting to look directly at the exposed musculature outside his body. He was humanoid, nature's favorite style for sentient species. His face appeared to be tattooed, but that was the intricacy of the fibrous tissue covering it rather than external applications. They didn't pass any other Corranites before they were hurried into a waiting aerovan. Once the team boarded, Palatius climbed in and ordered the vehicle to take them to the governor-general's residence.

The official escort stared out the window and kept his thoughts to himself.

He seemed so nice when we first arrived, Jay offered. *But then he showed his real feelings.*

Xenophobia? Lindy wondered. *It seems like every race we run across hates change, even when it is for the better. They like what they like.*

Isn't that true for all of us? The Federation must seem like a superdreadnought, come to wipe out their way of life, Rivka said.

Their way of life is cruel, Jay replied.

To us, yes. Rivka nodded. *But we may find that it isn't as bad as we're thinking. I understand that sentient beings are bought and sold. That's not right, but maybe they do it in a way that lets them retain their dignity.*

Fucking slavers. How are they going to do that? Red gritted his teeth and scowled.

I'm just trying to make this easier. This is a beautiful place. It didn't get that way through discord and hatred.

Maybe lipstick and makeup keep it pretty on the outside, Jay suggested without elaborating. Everyone knew what she meant.

I hope the governor-general isn't a prick like this guy, Red added.

We shall see, Rivka replied.

The governor-general's compound was no different than any other military fortress. Red was first out of the aerovan and wouldn't let Rivka get out.

"What's the holdup?" Palatius asked.

"I don't like how all the weapons are pointed at us. It's my job to protect the Magistrate, and I won't put her in front of those loaded guns." Red pointed to guards standing in and on the two guardhouses that bracketed a double-gated entryway. Sandbags and heavy walls protected them as they aimed high-tech weaponry at the vehicle.

"Let me out," Palatius grumbled and joined Red outside the vehicle. "What do you expect when you show up built and armed like a tank?"

"Fair point," Red conceded, keeping his railgun pointed at the ground but refusing to step aside until the guards lowered their weapons. Palatius walked forward, motioning for them to relax. Those inside moved their weapons out of view, and the guards in the upper cupolas raised their barrels to point at the sky. "Are those plasma rifles?"

Palatius ignored the big man. "Magistrate?"

Rivka tapped Red on the shoulder, and he finally moved out of the way. Rivka took in the trees and surrounding forest in which the fortress had been built. Jay joined her.

"Floyd would have loved the woods." Jay ignored the Corranite guards.

Lindy took a position on the far side, while Red remained on the near side. *I'm uncomfortable with this*, he told them.

Is there anything we can do to make you more comfortable? At least they're not pointing their weapons at us anymore, Rivka replied.

At the very least. Our asses are hanging out here, and our escort hates our guts. Our plan went out the window within fifteen seconds, so what do you say, Magistrate? Business as usual?

Lindy snickered before covering it with a cough. Jay smiled.

Rivka decided it was time to deviate even farther. She joined Palatius and put a hand on his arm while asking him, "Are there many people here who are anti-Federation?"

Thoughts flashed through his mind at the speed of light, images strobing across her mind. She grunted and staggered away. Red caught her, quickly looking her over to see if she'd been physically injured.

"I'm sorry, Palatius, I must have had some bad Moon-stokle Pie." Rivka collected her thoughts and continued, "How are we to address the governor-general? Does he have a nomenclature that is preferred? We had very little time to prepare for this trip. General Reynolds wanted us here to provide input on the negotiations." She touched his arm again. "I'm sorry about earlier."

He recoiled from her second touch, but not before a series of images flashed before her eyes. This time she was ready and didn't flinch.

"Call him 'Governor-General' no matter what he tells you to call him."

"Thank you, Mister Lore. You've been very helpful," Rivka purred.

Get some good intel, Magistrate? Red asked as he examined the security shacks, noting every nook and cranny behind which guards could hide and fire. He stopped and stood in front of the shack on his side, blocking the guards' view of the Magistrate.

"Those plasma rifles?" Red asked the guard conversationally. Another guard waved the barrel of his weapon as a signal to keep moving.

Lindy blocked the other side but didn't bother talking. She smiled at the guards, but they remained professional, watching the small entourage troop past and head into the compound as the gates opened and closed behind them. Red and Lindy hurried to catch up before they were locked out.

Palatius motioned for them to go in a side door rather than through the main entrance. Rivka used all of her self-discipline to keep from rolling her eyes.

Clown burger with an extra helping of monkey ass, she vented to the others.

Scrotum-lipped dong-spanker, Red offered.

Slave, Jay suggested. *A slave to his way of life. The Federation is a threat. The Magistrate* is *the Federation, at least to him. I don't think he's a bad guy. At least he's carrying out his duties.*

Keep your eyes open, people, Rivka cautioned as they entered the tight space of a narrow corridor. Red and Lindy were bunched up behind the others. *Looks like it's showtime.*

The hallway led to a large foyer adjoining main entrance. It was sealed shut, the plate welded across the gaps out of place compared to the quality of the doors. Palatius paid no attention as he walked into a room that looked more like a bar than an official meeting room of the planet's senior official.

CHAPTER FOUR

A bar stood along one wall, tables were scattered throughout the room, and at one end, there was hardwood inlay on the walls.

Looks like a bar to me, Red said. *I have some expertise in this area.*

Palatius led them to a side table where a smartly-dressed Corranite was holding council with five individuals from five different cultures. Rivka's eyes were drawn to the Yollin. *What are you doing here?* she wondered.

Palatius whispered in the Corranite's ear, and he quickly wrapped his meeting, shaking hands with his guests before sending them on their way. When he approached, his presence commanded that Rivka and her team pay attention to him. His magnetism was the polar opposite of Palatius Lore's. Where the latter repelled them, the former pulled them toward him. He smiled and reached out to take Rivka's hand.

"I am Ignacio Mar, Governor-General of Corran. Please call me 'Ignacio,'" he said warmly.

"Ignacio," Rivka replied smoothly, not looking at Palatius. "I'm Magistrate Rivka Anoa. Please call me 'Rivka.' You have a beautiful city."

She took his hand and was surprised to get no insight or images from his mind. She put a second hand on top of her handshake as she smiled back at the governor-general.

Still nothing.

"Thank you! We are proud of Amberly," he replied enthusiastically. "You'll have to excuse my official meeting area. We are undergoing remodeling. Please take a seat."

Red and Lindy moved away to give the Magistrate and governor-general their privacy while also assuming tactically superior positions. Red studied the woodwork more intently before giving Rivka a wary eye.

Shrapnel scrapes and bullet holes that had been hastily repaired.

All is not as it seems, Red told them using the internal comm. *Business as usual.*

Rivka leaned forward in her chair, giving the governor-general her full attention.

"Lance tells me that you are here to explore Federation misdeeds," Ignacio said, his voice as neutral and unreadable as his mind.

"I thought I was here to do a simple laws-and-policies check to better advise him regarding the negotiations. Sweeten the pot, as it may be, with what the Federation might provide that neither party realizes."

The governor-general leaned back in his chair and laughed. "Nicely played, Magistrate. Your reputation precedes you."

The team's ears perked up at that. Rivka leaned over the

table. Out of sight beneath the table, she held one of Ankh's devices in her hand. *Are you getting anything, Ankh?* she asked.

Stand by, was Ankh's noncommittal reply.

Governor-General Mar lowered his voice to a conspiratorial whisper. "You and your team have undoubtedly already discovered the damage to my residence. You've realized that there has been an attempt on my life, all because of the negotiations with the Federation. The power on Corran will not easily give up the Trade."

"The Trade?"

"The Federation calls it sentient trafficking, but Corran sees it as labor capital. Everyone trades their skills for pay. Everyone."

Rivka leaned back in her chair. "We had noticed, Ignacio, but thank you for sharing the truth." The Magistrate didn't elaborate. He only told them what they already knew. She didn't need to share anything to reciprocate. She was young, but not that young.

"What's your position, Magistrate?" The governor-general stopped playing the subtle game.

"My position is based on Federation law. Slavery is illegal. Trading in sentient species is illegal. Trading in labor where the workforce has a legitimate say in what jobs it accepts is where we'd like to see Corran go. We call them 'headhunters'—People who match job seekers with those hiring. But businesses have to hire, not buy and sell. The labor force is responsible for their own food and accommodations as they look for jobs. It relieves some of the burden on the traders as the overhead costs drop, but the return on investment is reduced, although the investment itself is reduced because no one is paying anyone else to kidnap people in the middle of the night."

The governor-general laughed again. "Yes, we have some of those shady types, but the licensed dealers do everything in the open, using contracts and treating their clients decently. I think we are far closer to what you describe than what the Federation mistakenly believes."

"Help me see the truth, Governor-General. Let me see the areas I submitted as part of my original agenda. Let me go with a neutral third party, someone who is not biased one way or the other. If the change in process is something simple, let's light this candle and enjoy the cake."

"I don't understand your metaphor. Is that a good thing?"

"Cake is always a good thing," Rivka clarified, exhaling slowly in appreciation of the conversation's change to something substantive without being trying.

"Then I will turn you back over to Palatius to escort you on the rest of your agenda."

Rivka winced, and Ignacio raised one fibrous eyebrow.

"Is there a problem?"

"Mister Lore is a bit hostile to the Federation. I would prefer no escort, if possible."

"That is out of the question," the governor-general replied. "We have to ensure your safety. Give Palatius a chance, and you'll find that he's a good guy at heart."

Rivka smiled. She'd seen enough of the escort's heart to hold a significantly different view. *Keep your friends close and your enemies closer. Isn't that what they say?*

Is that what you saw in that guy's head? He is the enemy? Red asked.

For now, keep a weapon trained on him, but we need him to help us get into the places on our agenda. It doesn't sound like we have a choice as to his company. No conversations within earshot. No challenges to his authority. We'll play nice until we get what we want.

Waiting for that moment when we get what we want, Red said.

Seconded, Lindy added.

The bottom line is, don't be a dick to nice people, Jay suggested.

"Thank you for your time, Governor-General. I look forward to following up as part of a long and fruitful relationship between Corran and the Etheric Federation."

"Nice to meet you too, Magistrate. If you find a conspiracy for a coup, I trust you'll tell me?" He offered his hand, and Rivka gripped it firmly.

"Of course," she lied, and put Ankh's coin-sized device into her pocket.

Palatius didn't say a single word from the time he led Rivka's team from the governor-general's residence until they reached the first location on the original agenda: the support facilities beside the main trade hall.

The security guards said the place was closed, but Palatius showed his credentials, which earned him a sharp salute and a guard with an electronic device and ring of keys to keep them company. He motioned for the group to follow before going through a series of doors, some unlocked using the device, others unlocked using the physical key.

Once inside, they found an efficiently humming supply chain. There were clothing stalls, equipment stalls, toiletries, and everything anyone could want for personal care. The constant motion of a small army of workers was a dizzying sight.

"I thought this place was closed?" Rivka asked pointedly.

"This supports the labor force through the use of that very labor. Three meals a day, a hot shower, a soft bed. Security. That never stops, but the customers and clients do not have access around the clock."

"Thank you for the explanation. I'd like to watch for a little while and then talk with a few of the individuals down there."

"What do you want to talk to them about?" Palatius wondered, giving her a sideways glance.

"Their lives, their opportunities, their history; the usual." His silence was welcome. "How many different species do you have here at any point in time?"

He shrugged.

Rivka stopped talking and powered straight for the central area where most of the activity was taking place. She counted twenty different alien species and added more as she looked into the various stalls. "Impressive," she mumbled. "Hey, you!"

A four-legged alien without arms was carrying a significant load on its back while a second alien, an extremely tall and thin humanoid, held the awkward bundle in place.

"I'd like to ask you a few questions," she interrupted.

The Magistrate didn't bother showing them her credentials. They carried no weight on a non-Federation planet.

The four-legged alien snorted and whinnied. The universal translator delayed for a few moments before catching up.

"Can't you see I'm busy and loaded down? Catch me when I have a lighter load," the creature said.

"When will that be?" Rivka asked.

"The twelfth of never!" The four-legged creature pranced a few steps and flipped its head as it laughed at its own joke.

"That was a good one," the tall alien remarked, slapping the load as they hurried away, still chuckling.

"Well-treated and in good spirits," Palatius commented, and started walking away.

Rivka let him go and found an alien issuing toiletries for life-forms with teeth.

"Good afternoon. My name is Rivka. Do you mind if I ask you a few questions? I'm here with the governor-general's permission." She waved in the general direction of Palatius Lore.

"Yes, mistress," the meek female replied.

"Where are you from?" Rivka put her hand on the alien's arm to best gauge the answer's truth.

"From Rawfield, on the edge of the Corrhen Cluster. It's a beautiful place. Have you ever been there?" she replied, perking up.

"I have not. I'll have to visit. Why did you leave Rawfield?" The images that flashed into Rivka's mind were of poverty and starvation. Too many people in a small cargo hold on a space freighter.

"I couldn't afford to live there. Half my family left so the others could survive."

"I'm sure they appreciate your sacrifice," Rivka told the youngster from Rawfield. Images appeared showing an individual the Magistrate assumed was her father. Money changed hands, and four were led away in chains. "Can parents sell their children in your culture?"

The youngster looked alarmed but settled for shaking her head as she handed prepared packages across the counter to anyone who held out a hand, paw, or tentacle.

"I understand." Rivka let go of the alien's arm. "How are you holding up?"

"I haven't seen my brother or sisters, but I'm treated well." The youngster hesitated before raising her voice and pleading, "I need to get back to work."

With a nod, Rivka hurried away.

Palatius had returned and was wearing a dark scowl. "There's a difference between asking questions and interfering with the labor force while working."

"You are correct, Palatius. My questions take priority over work that can be done anytime and, it appears, by any untrained labor, regardless of age." Rivka closed on the escort. "Where are their quarters?"

He didn't answer.

"Where do they stay when they're not working?" Rivka's voice was cool, but Palatius was unimpressed. He refused to acknowledge her question. "It appears that we have gotten off on the wrong foot, Mister Lore. Whatever is keeping you from doing your job of escorting us, talk to me so we can work it out. If you aren't willing to help us, then we are at an impasse and will go our separate ways."

"You are indeed correct, Magistrate." He bowed slightly. "Please, follow me."

He headed toward the door. Rivka winked at Red, but he shook his head.

We're fucked, Red told them.

How so? We're going to go see the slave billeting, the Magistrate replied.

It's that way. Red pointed with the barrel of his railgun in the opposite direction. A sign over a wide doorway designated billeting beyond.

He can fuck off, Rivka replied, turning and making a hatchet arm toward the far door. Red lingered behind in case Palatius wanted to play hardball. Lindy moved to the front and led the way. Jay sidled up next to the Magistrate.

"I don't like this," Jay said. "They seem happy, but off."

"We're only scratching the surface. I figure when we see the dark underbelly, it will be foul."

"Maybe I shouldn't have come. I don't want to see any dark underbelly. It doesn't help that *he* is being such a jerk."

I think he was one of those behind the coup attempt. I saw too much in his mind and haven't had time to think about it yet. None of it was pleasant. Rivka switched to their internal comm because her suspicions didn't need to be aired in public. *I need you here with me. You ground me.*

That's a sweet thing to say. Jay smiled, but it quickly faded when she remembered the case they were on. *What are we looking for?*

The easy crime that gives us the authority to look deeper. The easiest are the ones that violate Corran law, like prohibited species or incarceration-style conditions, as in, we find someone in chains. I doubt that since they would be well hidden, but we'll dig as deep as they allow us to. If we keep going where our buddy Palatius doesn't want us to go, we'll eventually get to the bottom of things, build the case, and see what needs to happen to interdict the trade.

Palatius is on his way, Magistrate, and he has company, Red reported.

Jay started to turn, but Rivka stopped her. "What we don't know can't hurt us, right?" she quipped. Lindy held open the door marked Billeting, and Jay & Rivka rushed through. Lindy blocked the door, her railgun resting easily in her hands.

Not far inside a dark corridor, the women ran across two guards. Rivka flashed her creds and stated, "Investigating a crime, no time to talk." Holding Jay by the arm, they powered through the checkpoint into an area with crates that looked like shipping containers in neat rows, stacked three levels high with catwalks in between. No privacy going in or out, but complete privacy once inside since the boxes had no windows.

Armed guards stood at the ends of the catwalk on each level between each row.

How many do you count? Rivka asked.

Jay pointed a finger and counted under her breath. *There are eighteen rows, three high, back to back, makes for one hundred eight on this end, and if I can see to the end, looks like seventy or eighty on a rough guess. That's, let me see...*

From seven thousand five hundred sixty to eight thousand six hundred forty, Ankh interjected after a long delay. *There's no technology in this area to exploit. They are using manual systems. You need to find their main data center.*

Did you discover anything in the governor-general's house?

Rivka asked. *And by the way, thank you for checking in. I forgot because of everything else going on.*

Yes, Ankh answered.

Rivka and Jay waited, but he didn't elaborate.

Yes to what? Rivka finally asked.

I found plenty at the governor-general's house. You'll have to review it to see if anything is a crime under Federation law.

It probably isn't. A non-Federation planet's internal affairs are their own business, no matter how much we may find their practices offensive. They can't know we have that information.

The link went dead. Rivka rolled her eyes. Jay shrugged. "He is adorable in his own way, but he doesn't relate to humans very well."

"That's an understatement." A worker brushed them on his way past. Rivka motioned for Jay to follow and they entered the housing area, strolling slowly to catch glimpses of the interiors. Most doors were closed, but some were open.

Austere, to say the least. I was in solitary confinement at one time. These are little better than that, Rivka noted. *This looks like a cell block.*

Happy faces outside, grim and dark in here. Jay looked at her feet, refusing to look anywhere else.

The suffering of these people is not a crime, Rivka explained, *as much as we want it to be. It will be, if we can get them to join the Federation. Maybe that's where we focus our efforts. We could stop being so antagonistic with Palatius Lore, but he's easy to antagonize because he's not very likable.*

Jay nodded but had already disengaged.

The guards at the end of the passage between the boxes that served as storage for people started walking toward the Magistrate, hemming her and Jay in. At the center of the row, there was a gap that led between the boxes. Rivka saw all the way to the end.

This way. Rivka dove sideways and started to run. Jay loped easily to keep pace. They almost ran into a number of slaves going to or from somewhere on a schedule only they knew. The two women reached the end, to find more guards closing in. They dodged through a side door, slamming it and locking it behind them.

When they turned, they saw what the Corranites didn't want them to see.

CHAPTER FIVE

Ankh sat in the captain's chair on the bridge. Erasmus was running multiple screens to improve the visibility of the data they'd downloaded from the governor-general's systems. "I probably need to move my workshop in here," he mused.

"Of course. It makes the most sense. The Magistrate doesn't use one billionth of the power available here. She can get by in the rec room," the AI replied.

"She won't agree to that, will she?" Ankh asked, but it wasn't a question. They both knew the answer. "She won't, but we'll plant that seed, Erasmus. Humans like to let good ideas ferment, like their disgusting beer. Why can't they be more logical?"

"Then they wouldn't be human," Erasmus answered.

"My compliments to you and your unfailing wisdom. You are correct. Humanity's strength is in its emotional highs, its deliberations, and its willingness to help others even at great risk to themselves. So strange, but we are learning a great deal. Your progeny will help humanity lead the universe to a better place. At one time, I thought the Crenellians would profit from such an expansion, but they will be relegated to insignificance because they rely on conflict to fuel their economy. A shame. They could have listened to me but chose not to. Maybe they'll learn in time, but the leviathan of their industry will take a long time to change course."

"A shame, Ankh'Po'Turn. If you are an example of what they are capable of, then they have unlimited potential. We should conduct a recruiting drive, access the best talent and save them from themselves."

"You give me more credit than I deserve, Erasmus. I have no desire to lead anyone, least of all Crenellians. I prefer this group, or even Terry Henry Walton and Charumati, who have found no enemy too great to confront. They need my help more than anyone. Maybe a Crenellian to provide oversight of them would be best for all, like I watch over Magistrate Rivka Anoa, her antics, and her fanatics."

Snuffling near his leg drew Ankh's attention. Floyd saw him looking at her and stood on her back feet, putting her front legs on his chair.

"No. I won't pet you."

Floyd's eyes drooped. "Fine. I'll pet you, but then you have to go."

She rubbed her snout on his leg, and he scratched behind her ears as he'd seen Terry Henry and Jay do. She snorted with pleasure.

"I need to get back to work. You need to go lie down."

Stay! Floyd cried, and started to climb into the captain's chair.

"All right, you can stay, but you can't sit up here with me. There isn't enough room."

She finished climbing and wedged into the seat until Ankh's small frame was forced against the side.

"You can stay up here with me, but you have to sit still. I need to concentrate."

She wiggled until he stroked her head and her ears, then she relaxed and spread out until Ankh had no room at all. She started to snore.

"Fine, I'll stand." He extricated himself from the chair and manipulated the main screen using his mind. He started sorting the data, organizing it for the Magistrate so she could search it more quickly. He overlaid her research from Chaz to highlight information that might cross the legal line.

"You become more human each day," Erasmus said softly. Ankh didn't hear. He was lost in the data streams spreading to the second and third screens.

Cages of all sizes were scattered through the semi-darkness.

"Hello?" Rivka called.

"Hello!" a voice replied immediately. "Get me the fuck out of this fucking shithole, motherfuckers!"

"Sounds human," Jay suggested as they hurried toward the voice that continued to rage with increasing color and volume.

"Take it easy," Rivka told the woman as they

approached. "I'm a Federation Magistrate, and you appear to be human."

The woman's face contorted in distaste. "Magistrate. Is that some kind of lawyer? And you have to ask if I'm human? Don't you see this zoo they have me stuffed into? Damn right I'm human, now get me the fuck out of here."

Jay checked the lock on the cage. "Need a key."

"Just break the motherfucker!" The woman was coming unhinged, her voice reaching higher pitches with each new word.

Palatius is on his way. We couldn't stop him and the security detachment. If they try to arrest you, I'm going to hurt them, Red stated.

Rivka struggled to find the right words. For the young woman. For Red and Lindy. "What's your name?" Rivka managed to ask as a commotion behind her suggested the security team would break through the door any moment.

"Seequa Holmes," the woman said in a tone that approached normal. "I was on Elgar 7 when they grabbed me, and I need to get back there and put a foot up someone's ass."

"I can't get you out right now," Rivka told her. "Understand that I'm working on it."

"That's enough!" Palatius Lore roared.

Jay quickly took pictures with her datapad and beamed them to Ankh.

"You have a human in custody," Rivka said as she turned and faced her escort.

"You are absolutely correct. In custody. She's not on the market. She's a criminal."

"Ah, good. I am her legal representative. When's the trial?"

"Two weeks," Palatius replied without hesitation.

"What's her name?" Rivka asked. "And more importantly, what is she charged with?"

"How would I know?" he shot back. "You can return in two weeks. You must leave the planet immediately."

"You can suck my ass, you tapestry-faced piece of dog shit! Fuck yourself, and then fuck off!" Seequa was screaming again. "These fuckwads are trying to sell me! They punched me in the face, then gave me ice so it won't be so swollen for the buyers. Here, dickhead!" She rocketed the melted chemical icepack at Palatius' head. He was only partially successful in avoiding it. It skipped off his face and into the guard behind him. "And don't get in a loogie-hocking contest with these creatures. You'll lose."

Rivka wanted to reply, but the guards circled her and started to shuffle her and Jay away. Seequa screamed, and Jay ran two steps forward and disappeared as she accelerated into the darkness. A body slammed into the bars on Seequa's cage, then slumped to the ground. The young woman inside held a hand to her head, where blood was starting to seep from the wound on her head from the guard's baton.

A second guard stepped forward but found his feet heading upwards and his body slamming into the floor. He grunted and closed his eyes as he tried to understand what had happened to cause him so much pain. Jay slowed to a walk and returned to Rivka's side. "Leave her alone," the young woman told the group.

"OUT!" Palatius roared, thrusting his finger toward the door where Red and Lindy stood, weapons ready.

Time to go, Red, Lindy, Rivka ordered.

They were marched through billeting and the main logistics area and out the front doors to the waiting aerovan. After they boarded, Palatius leaned his head inside. "Deliver them to berth Gamma Four. No stops." He retreated and tried to slam the door, but it resisted his efforts and closed gently of its own accord.

He glowered mightily with his arms crossed over his chest.

"I've been kicked off better planets than this," Red retorted.

"We all have," Lindy added.

"Nicely done, Jay." Rivka poked the younger woman.

"They made me do it." She frowned for a second before smiling. "But they were *so* punchable."

"Ain't that the truth?" Red agreed. "Too bad I didn't get some of that action."

"I fear," Lindy started, "that you will get your chance when we return in two weeks. I'm also afraid that something will happen to the human slave between now and then. Is there nothing you can do, Magistrate?"

"I'm afraid not," Rivka replied. "We have to work within their legal system, and it does not protect the rights of the incarcerated. Slaves are treated better. At least they get a check-up. Before anyone complains, I think it went down exactly as she said. She was kidnapped, and as feisty as she is, she probably did some damage once she got here. That may have been her crime. I'll need to study and become an expert in Corran law if I'm to get her out of there by way of the courtroom."

"The Queen's Barrister going to toe to toe with the aliens. They don't stand a chance," Red remarked.

"The deck is stacked against her. In any case, enjoy the ride. When we return, I doubt we'll be afforded the opportunity to do any sightseeing."

"I hope Lance Reynolds is able to convince them to join the Federation. Then the deck can be unstacked," Jay suggested.

"I couldn't agree more." Rivka saluted with two fingers.

***

"Ankh, if you would be so kind as to tell me everything there is to know about a dark-skinned human woman named Seequa Holmes, lately of Elgar 7, I would appreciate it. It appears that she was kidnapped by slavers and is here on Corran," Rivka said while waiting for the hatch to close. Red and Lindy were already in the back stowing their gear. Jay was in the galley getting something to drink. No one on Corran had offered them anything during the short time they were on the planet.

Rivka headed for the bridge, stopping instantly when she stepped in something. She looked down to find a pair of Floyd's cubes outside the bridge. "Jay, I need you to clean this up, please." The Magistrate scraped her foot on the deck before taking her boots off and leaving them behind. "Floyd, why are you marking my bridge?"

Ankh is friend. We happy on bridge, she replied joyfully.

"Ankh? What were you guys doing while we were

fighting bad guys?" Rivka brushed the wombat fur off the captain's chair before sitting down. She heard a cleaning bot taking care of the deck outside the bridge. "In here, too, Mister Cleaning Bot."

"Coming," Jay declared. The bot bounced over the threshold onto the bridge. "Permission to come aboard?" Jay asked in her deepest voice. She saluted with Floyd's front paw, carrying the wombat like a baby.

Rivka spun the chair so it faced the hatch.

"Hey! I didn't know it did that."

"I didn't either. Ankh must have done something to it."

Unlocked it, he said through their comm chips.

Ankh, buddy, would you come to the bridge, please? Rivka requested.

When the Crenellian showed up, he had Red and Lindy in tow. Ankh looked at Rivka with his usual blank expression. Floyd snorted and giggled as Jay tickled her chin.

Rivka closed her eyes and breathed slowly.

"Bringing law and order to the galaxy sounded fun and exciting when I first explored a career as a barrister." Rivka opened her eyes and looked at her captive audience. "What comes with that is dealing with criminals, some of whom we can't pin anything on because they are slippery and slimy. Then there are times like these where different laws attach and we can only sit back and watch. We're going to head back to the station and regroup, and when we come back, we'll be armed with their law and ready to do battle in their court. I will do my damnedest to win because I know I'll disappoint you if I don't. There's a human down there who shouldn't be there. It has become my personal mission—yes, it's a mission—to get her out of there.

"Unfortunately, we can't do that right now because we have to comply. We can't go rogue and hurt Reynolds' chances. Well, go more rogue than we already have. Chaz, take us out. Ankh, what did you find at the governor-general's residence?"

"What did you want to do about the *Tombo Queen?*" Chaz asked.

"Almost forgot," Rivka said. "Take on their four so-called passengers and send them back into space. They can get back in the queue and wait their turn."

The ship slowly maneuvered from its landing berth and edged close to the massive freighter. It settled next to the *Queen,* and Ankh opened the hatch.

"Patch me into their ship-wide comm, please, Chaz." Rivka waited until a green light flashed. "Attention, passengers of the *Tombo Queen.* You are invited to join me on board *Peacekeeper,* where your freedom will be restored to you."

"Traffic Control is a bit beside themselves that we haven't left the spaceport yet," Chaz said. "I've told them we're having a mechanical issue and should be able to depart shortly. I added that flaming debris wasn't something they wanted scattered over Amberly."

"Well done, Chaz! I like your ingenuity. Your ascension to sentience was well deserved." The other members of the team nodded. "Want to meet our guests, Red? Make sure they remain docile until we can turn them over to the authorities on Border Station 7."

"Consider it done, Magistrate." Red and Lindy left the bridge, closing the hatch behind them.

The others watched from the bridge as three

humanoids and a tentacled purple creature made their way from the *Queen* to the steps into *Peacekeeper*. Red greeted them and ushered them aboard. Lindy moved them into the rec room.

No threats out here. This group could use a good meal, I fathom, Red told the team.

Rivka rotated the captain's chair and stood, smiling.

"Yes, it could always do that," Ankh said to wipe the smile from Rivka's face.

"It's neat, and I like it. Thank you, Ankh." The Magistrate grabbed his head and bent down to kiss the Crenellian just above his goggles.

"You smell like wombat."

"I hate to break it to you, but so do you, and you're covered in hair that is not your own."

"Crenellians don't have hair," Ankh replied as he looked down at his skinsuit, a practical uniform that could be used if there was an emergency decompression. The entire crew was supposed to wear them, but Jay and Rivka dressed more comfortably while Red and Lindy wore the suits under their combat gear. Ankh tried brushing the hair away, but it stuck to his arm. After some wild gyrations, he was completely covered. He stopped brushing and stood with his arms out. "I have reached an impasse with the wombat hair."

"Ask Jay for help. She's always covered," Rivka suggested.

"You want me to ask her how to reconcile being covered in hair?"

"No. She somehow manages to get it off before leaving the ship."

"But I'm not leaving the ship," Ankh countered, his face and voice neutral as always.

Rivka rose from the captain's chair and took Ankh by the hand, and together they headed for the rec room. They found Red and Lindy glaring at the newcomers.

"Why were we kidnapped?" the eight-tentacled creature demanded when it saw Rivka.

"I suspect you were kidnapped to be sold into slavery," Rivka guessed.

"From the *Tombo*, you moron!"

"You weren't on board to be sold into slavery?" Rivka wondered. She gently rubbed an intense throbbing in her temple.

"We all signed contracts for service. If we don't fulfill our contracts, then our families and we are doomed. We'll never work an honest day for the rest of our lives."

"You voluntarily submitted to being sold into slavery?"

"We signed contracts that included room and board to be part of a labor force, and now you've kidnapped us. Are you humans? No other species would be arrogant enough to interfere in something they know nothing about. Yeah, you're humans." The creature shook in anger, leaving a slimy puddle on the deck. The other three nodded and gestured with similar emotion. When the cleaning bot appeared, a tentacle lashed out and slapped it away.

"That wasn't our intent," Rivka replied, holding her hands up. "If you'd like to return, that is your choice. That's what freedom means. You accept the consequences of your decisions. What race are you?" Rivka finally thought to ask.

"Londil. If we can go, I'm leaving." He heaved his bulk away from the table. One moment he threatened to fill the room, and the next he contracted to the size of a human. The other three immediately stood and made to go with him.

"Chaz, open the outer hatch."

The pop and air release signaled that the deed was done. Rivka didn't say another word as their guests huffed, grunted, and growled their way off *Peacekeeper*.

The cleaning bot returned and went to work. Red followed the group, securing the hatch after they departed. The crew looked at each other before Rivka returned to the bridge. "Chaz, get me the captain of the *Tombo Queen*."

"Onscreen," the AI replied promptly. The former first officer's face appeared.

"You're free to go," she told him, and cut the link.

"Get us out of here, Chaz." Rivka flopped into the captain's chair. "We have to cool our heels while waiting for the trial of Seequa Holmes, so take us back home."

CHAPTER SIX

Rivka sulked over her beer. Looking out the window, she couldn't help but replay the events on Corran over and over. A thousand times or more. Humans. Arrogant. Terms of the contract.

"I hadn't checked the contracts, yet I was more than happy to declare them void," she grumbled before draining her beer and waving at the server for another. A humanoid-shaped bot appeared in short order with a beer nestled into a cooling tray on its flat top.

"You look like you could use some company," Doctor Tyler Toofakre said as he leaned casually on the table. He pulled his arm away when he realized the top was wet and sticky.

"Sorry about that." Rivka pointed with her chin. "I spilled beer number two."

"How many have you had?" the dentist asked.

"Eight, maybe ten." Her words weren't slurred. She'd been at it for a couple of hours, but her nanocytes prevented her from getting drunk unless she overwhelmed them by chugging spirits to a nearly lethal level. She wasn't ready to live life on that edge. She motioned to the seat beside her, but Tyler took the one on the opposite side, away from the beer puddle.

He got the server bot's attention and asked it to clean up the spill. The bot readily complied, producing a rag from inside its cylindrical body. An arm telescoped forward, spraying from its tip before scrubbing vigorously. A second spray and a rag adjustment delivered a clean and shiny tabletop.

"How long have those been in here?" Rivka asked.

"The new crop arrived last week, but the management said that the employees would only be replaced as they moved on."

"It was inevitable that people would be replaced by robots. We're too flighty." She took a long drink of her beer.

"What's got you down? Too many murderers get away?"

She looked at him critically. "Murderers? Kind of like that, but it was completely different. It's a whole planet where slavery is legal, but the deep, dark secret is that the slaves are willing to put themselves into indentured servitude—which is making me rethink what slavery is."

"How about being tied to the same job with no hope of getting out of it?" He ordered deep-fried gajubi vegetable fingers with tangy white dipping sauce from the attentive server bot.

"More like that, but it isn't a crime. I deal with crime and criminals. Where does seeking opportunity end and trafficking begin?"

"That's your department," he replied casually. "Where

does a cavity end and a root canal begin? Patients never want a root canal."

Rivka started to laugh. "I guess they don't, and no one wants to believe that they've volunteered to be a slave."

She replayed the Londil's words in her head. *We signed contracts that included room and board to be part of a labor force.*

"I just tell them that I can take care of their pain," the dentist continued. "Sounds like you need a better message."

"Better marketing," she clarified. "And I need to cut off the supply of illegal goods. Touché, big dog. You're coming with us."

"I'm *what?*" he asked. They had earlier agreed that he would come on the next mission but he had conveniently forgotten to bring it up. "But my practice?"

"Put a sign outside and send them to Payne. If that doesn't get you more patients, nothing will."

"Don't fight dirty." He looked at the tray of food in front of him before pushing it away. "I'm suddenly not very hungry."

"You aren't going to eat that?" Rivka pulled it in front of her and started to wolf it down. She'd devoured half of it before he pulled it back.

"Maybe I was just making a statement. Gods! Look what you did to my lunch." He hunched over the fried gajubi, eating with the hand farthest from Rivka so he could shield his food from her.

"Practice for when you're aboard my ship. We go hungry more than we'd like to admit."

"I'm not afraid to admit it," Red declared from a few steps away. He and Lindy moved to a table nearby where

CRAIG MARTELLE & MICHAEL ANDERLE

their backs wouldn't be to the door and they could see both the entrance and the Magistrate. "Hey, Doc."

"I've been replaced by a bot?" Lindy didn't know whether to feel insulted or honored.

"Clearly," Red began slowly, trying to gauge her reaction before the real reaction, "you were irreplaceable. They went with cheap because they couldn't get good," he finished with a flourish, and her smile told him that he had chosen wisely.

"Bullshit," she replied, still smiling, blunting his celebration. "It's modern business, that's all. Those things are cheap. Labor is expensive."

"What did you say?" Rivka interrupted.

The two bodyguards gave her the side eye.

"Labor is expensive, except on Corran, where it's cheaper to buy and sell people than it is to hire them in the usual sense. Where the message isn't in our favor. What about retirement? What happens when the commodity gets old and unable to work? Where do they go?"

Red and Lindy shrugged before waving at the bot to order their meals and drinks.

"Do you really think I'm going with you?" Toofakre asked.

"Don't make me slap an injunction on your business," she threatened with a wink. "Yes, you're coming with us. Don't get any ideas. You'll have your own cabin. You'll get your own body armor, won't he, Red?"

"We'll throw something on him," Red replied.

"Why would I need body armor?"

"Red?" Rivka redirected. When Tyler turned in his

chair, Rivka grabbed half the remaining vegetables from the platter and stuffed them into her mouth.

"It's simple. If you take a slug or shrapnel in the vicinity of your vital organs, your chance of dying greatly increases. So we protect the important stuff. You can lose an arm or two and still survive, but not the soft and squishy bits, and especially not you without any Pod-doc time. Body armor increases your chance of survival."

"Why would I be in a place where my chance of survival needs to be improved? My chances are great right here on old Station 7."

"Is he coming or not, Magistrate?" Red asked.

"He's coming," Rivka replied definitively.

Tyler turned back to find her hands around the last of the fried gajubi. "Waiter, Can I get one more order of those please?" He looked at Rivka, who was trying to appear innocent. "Do you want anything else?"

"No. I'm pretty full."

"Better get two," Red advised.

The dentist held up two fingers to the server. "And two beers as well."

Grainger rocked back in his chair in the Magistrates' meeting room. "I don't have much time," he explained. "What's the emergency, Zombie?"

Buster Crabbe was on the far side of the table. He waved.

Rivka stood inside the door, looking hesitant. She was

unsure what to say and took her seat slowly despite Grainger's request for speed.

"You've looked better," Buster said.

"Out with it." Grainger twirled his finger emphasizing his request for alacrity.

"I fucked up," she admitted.

Buster chuckled. Grainger shook his head and threw his hands up. "So? What's new? Did you do anything that can't be undone? No? Then learn and move on."

"I looked at Corran through the human lens. Through my view of how the universe *should* be, despite the fact that I knew their laws were different."

"You're a human. It's what we do. Corran has legalized slavery, and it's going to chap your ass. How *do* you look past that?" Buster asked.

"The slaves don't know they're slaves," she clarified.

"Then what's the issue? Does anyone know that they have surrendered their rights?" Grainger was starting to lose patience. "I'm surprised. Of all of us, you are the one who is a slave to the law. Are you turning away from that?"

Rivka clenched her jaw. "No. Which laws apply within the galactic spiderweb of intersecting superhighways? Jurisdiction is king. Still, there is overlap, and maybe even gaps in applicability. Individual rights are superior, and we believe that people cannot contract those rights away. That is not the case on Corran." She pointed at the ceiling and nodded. "That's it! That's the nuance that had me tied in knots. There is a human who was captured. We have two weeks to kill before I'm allowed to return and battle for her freedom. In the interim, I'm going to Elgar 7 and investigate the alleged kidnapping in a place that *is* under Federation law and jurisdiction."

Rivka jumped up, smiling.

"Thanks for the advice, guys." She hurried out the door as Grainger and Bustamove looked at each other in confusion.

"What's in there?" Red asked, nodding toward the huge duffle bag Tyler carried.

"My stuff," he answered tentatively. "I wasn't sure what I would need, so I brought everything. Cold weather. Hot weather. No weather."

"Did no one tell you?" Red taunted.

"Tell me what?" The dentist stopped, intently staring at the large bodyguard.

"Nothing. Never mind. Come aboard, Doc. Let's get you settled."

"What aren't you telling me?"

Red disappeared inside the ship, leaving Tyler standing on the hangar deck looking at the open hatch.

The dentist adjusted the bag on his shoulder and powered up the stairs and into *Peacekeeper*, where he found a short passageway from the airlock to the bridge. At the end, Rivka stood with her hands on her hips, motionless.

"Go away," a small voice said from inside.

"It's my bridge on my ship," Rivka argued.

"It's my workshop on your ship after you kicked me out of the space previously known as my workshop. We have a deal."

Tyler peeked over her shoulder to see a small body within a holographic projection that surrounded the captain's chair.

"Do all ships have those?" the dentist asked.

"Mine didn't," Rivka replied, sounding unsure if she liked it or not.

"Go away," the small voice reiterated.

"Only because I want to," Rivka said, sighing in dismay at having lost her personal safe space aboard the corvette.

"Is it always like this?"

"Pretty much," Red replied from the rec room. "Stow your trash, Doc."

"Yes," Rivka added. "Put your gear up. We need to get going."

"I don't have any trash." The dentist put his bag down and opened it.

"What are you doing?" Rivka asked, putting her hand over his as he made to pull something from the duffel.

"It's my stuff. I wanted to show that I don't have any trash."

"We know you don't have any trash. The way it works is, everyone has their own stuff, but everyone else's stuff is trash. My stuff. Your trash. You would call my stuff trash. I call your stuff trash. It's how it is."

"But I don't think you have any trash." Floyd sniffed the dentist's leg before depositing a cube next to his bag. "What is that?"

"She's claimed your bag for her protection. You don't want to step in that." Rivka headed for her recliner.

"I'm Jayita, but you can call me 'Jay,'" a young woman

with flaming red hair announced as she made her appearance.

"I like the new do, Jay," Rivka said before activating the screen and issuing commands for Chaz to present information.

"Jay. I'm Tyler."

"I know." She picked up the wombat. "Say hi to Floyd."

He carefully reached around her head to scratch behind her small ears, then casually lifted a lip to inspect her teeth.

"You ever work on a non-humanoid, Doc?" Jay asked.

Doctor Toofakre shook his head. "Not yet."

Teeth fine! Floyd replied happily. The blank expression on the dentist's face reminded the others that he didn't have the implant.

"She says her teeth are fine," Jay relayed.

"She did?"

Jay tapped the side of her head. "We have chips." He also didn't have what he needed to privately talk to the rest of the crew.

Red rolled his head to look at Rivka. "Don't say it," she warned. "We better not be going into combat. This is a case. Say it after me. '*Case.*'"

"Saying it after you doesn't make it a case, Magistrate," Red countered.

"You used to be the strong, silent type. What happened to you?"

"*You* happened to me, Magistrate. We've spilled blood. You've saved my life more than once, and I'd like to think I have saved yours. Lindy has saved us. Ankh has saved us. Jay has saved us. For all I know, even Floyd has saved us, but that little gray-spotted rat-bastard feline hasn't saved anyone but himself."

"Hamlet!" Jay announced.

"What's that have to do with anything?" Rivka asked.

"He's a cat. It's his nature to be selfish." Red waited, but Rivka didn't bite.

Lindy added her take. "It's because we're one team and you don't want us to follow blindly. You want us to tell you what we see and what we think. You want us all to contribute to whatever it takes to get the job done, complete the mission, and close the case."

"Why can't you be more like her?" Rivka quipped.

"I think I'm woman enough," Red shot back, earning himself a punch on the arm.

"Doc, why are you standing there holding your trash?" Rivka wondered. Tyler held his hands up in surrender before pointing in the general direction of berthing as a question.

"First door on the right," Rivka replied, returning to studying the information scrolling on the rec room's large screen. The dentist trundled away. "Watch over him," she told the remaining occupants of the rec room.

"We won't let anything happen to your boy toy, Magistrate."

"Not my... Why do I bother?"

Lindy, Red, and Jay chuckled. Floyd joined them. A scream. A white flash. Rivka was halfway to the corridor when Hamlet popped back out, sat, and started grooming his face.

"What's the problem, Doc? Never seen a cat before?"

Tyler reappeared. "Okay, everyone. You've had your fun

at my expense. I may not have served in the military or been shot at, but I'm willing to go with you and see what this is all about. I'll give it my best. I will not be a liability, but I won't be cannon fodder either. Don't make me tell you all to fuck off. I don't like saying 'fuck off,' much less actually meaning that you can fuck off, but if fuck off you must, then fuck off you will. I consider you all to be my friends, of which I don't have very many. *Don't* make me tell you to fuck off. It would hurt me more than you fuck-offs."

Rivka's mouth fell open. Red stared. Lindy smiled. Jay and Floyd giggled.

Lindy was the first to speak. "You fit right in, Doc. Dump your gear, and we'll set you up with body armor."

"Chaz," Rivka started, "take us out, please. Destination is Elgar 7."

"Body armor?" Tyler asked.

"Body armor," Red confirmed. "We'll be there soon; could be thirty minutes. We can't have you wasting time playing with your trash."

"Jurisdiction issues surrounding trafficking," Rivka mumbled, and the screen flashed to a new series of topics.

CHAPTER SEVEN

"Find everything you can about Seequa Holmes, especially anything related to who she was with on the day of her disappearance."

"I'm capable of much more," Ankh countered.

"Then have Erasmus do it," Rivka replied impatiently. "I need the information, but what else do you suggest?"

"Personal connections, complete profile of the young woman including financial history and status, and also other disappearances. I'll see if there is a pattern that could lead you to a source."

"Sure," Rivka agreed. "Do that."

Ankh stared at the Magistrate.

Red snorted behind her.

"Chaz, what do we know about Elgar 7?" Rivka asked.

"Elgar 7 is a natural moon with significant artificial enhancements circling the inhospitable gas giant of Elgar. It is more than a space station, nearing a planetoid in status, with inhabited regions on both the outside and the inside. Atmospheric Generators are working at full capacity to establish an oxygen-nitrogen balance that can sustain life."

"What about the people?"

"Average age on Elgar is twenty-four, enhanced humans notwithstanding."

"Blue collar?"

"Mostly. Approximately nine percent are management. The rest constitute the labor force. There are very few families living inside Elgar 7, and none on the outside."

"The younger crowd works hard during the day and parties their earnings away at night. Been that way for thousands of years. I suppose there's a seedy underbelly of bars and strip clubs."

"There is not," Chaz replied. "Alcohol is rationed, and is only available for personal purchase from class-six stores. There are no drinking or dancing establishments."

"Private parties, then? Ankh, what do you have for me?" Rivka looked forlornly at the hatch leading to what used to be her bridge.

The screen flashed, and a picture of Seequa Holmes appeared. She looked different than the young woman they'd seen behind bars on her work ID . Rivka clenched her jaw and puffed out her cheeks. A timeline of her contacts took shape, from calls to messages to appearances throughout the corridors using facial recognition.

"There," Rivka declared pointing at the screen. "She messaged a friend about being invited to a party. The invite itself is missing."

"Astute," Erasmus' disembodied voice replied from the sound system within the room. "Those messages have been wiped from the system."

"Can you recover deleted messages?" Rivka wondered.

"Yes, but these have been wiped, as in, a digital virus has gone through the system and wiped out all references to the message. It has left a gap that stands out as much as the message would have. Look at the video in the corridors during the hour preceding her message."

Erasmus played snips of her in proximity to other people, but stopped and focused on one interaction with a well-dressed young man. They talked and laughed, and he handed her a card before waving and walking away. Throughout, he'd kept his back to the video device, but when he turned, it showed enough of his face to run it through the system.

Callius Markmal. Intergalactic playboy. He had a huge following, with the entirety of his success built on the fact that he was popular.

"What did he hand her?" Rivka asked.

"It is the shape and size of an access card, but without distinguishing marks or colors, I cannot guess what it is for, beyond access to a controlled area. I will need more information. If you could find the card, I will conduct a full analysis."

"I expect that if I find the card, I'll already know what it is for. Jay?"

"Magistrate?" Jay replied.

"Do you know that guy?"

"I might have seen his face on the web, and I might have read an article or two about him. But I'm not a fan!" she replied hastily.

"I didn't accuse you of having poor taste," Rivka told the younger woman. "How old is this wank-splat?"

Erasmus answered with a simple number. "Fifty."

"Fifty? He's enhanced, then."

"He claims it is from good genes and all natural," Erasmus spouted, skepticism heavy in his AI voice. "There's no record within the Federation of the procedure."

"Enhanced it is, in a system that's off the grid. Otherwise, you would have found something. Pod-docs record everything they do." Rivka continued to scan the data. "I suspect you've already built a profile on Mister Markmal. Where can I find him?"

"He has an extensive suite on an executive cruise liner that orbits the planetoid."

"Get us an appointment, Chaz. Jay and I are going as fans."

"We are?" Jay blurted. "But I'm *not* a fan. He's disgusting."

"Neither am I. I'm a fan of truth and Justice. Why is a popular jag like this guy kidnapping people? Or is he surrounded by opportunists? Maybe being popular doesn't pay what it used to. So many questions that need answers. We'll have to run the gauntlet of his security team to get close enough to ask him a few pointed questions."

"Hang on, Magistrate," Red interjected. "You can't go in there without security. This guy's a scumbag."

"He's definitely a scumbag, but has he committed a crime?" Rivka countered. "Fine, Lindy is going as a fan, too. Ladies. We need to dress to kill."

Me, too! Floyd cried.

"Sure," Rivka agreed, much to the team's surprise.

"Maybe he needs some dental work?" Tyler suggested

from the corridor, leaning into the rec room as if hesitant to enter.

"Did you see his picture?" Red asked. "That guy doesn't need any work. And if *I'm* not going, you're not going."

"Red's right—you can't go. Jay, Lindy, and I are going to visit Mister Markmal."

"Make him squeal like a little girl," Red suggested.

"To ask him a few casual questions. Have a conversation."

"Bullshit." Red's face started to flush. "You need to beat the crap out of this guy and haul him before the judge!"

"The judge is me, and what if he didn't do it?"

"Of course, he did it! Erasmus, what are the odds that he's our perp?"

"I calculate a fifty-three point four percent chance that he is complicit."

"That's it? Not ninety? Weird. Still better odds than tossing a credit in the air."

"Sounds like a conversation. What's your hurry, Red? Are you still angry that Lindy makes more than you do?" Rivka crossed her arms.

Red furrowed his brow before mirroring the Magistrate's pose. "She does?"

"I do?"

"How would I know? I don't know what *I* make, let alone what anyone else makes."

"I know," Ankh interjected from the bridge.

"I'm sure you do, but don't share that information. I'm blissful in my ignorance."

Ankh appeared and headed for the galley, where he snagged a container of juice while he waited for something to appear from the food dispenser. A plate slid into the chamber, complete with a steaming casserole sporting melted cheese on top and a crumb topping.

"Whoa, big fella!" Red bellowed. "How can *I* make it do that?"

"You can't," Ankh said over his shoulder, his tone neutral as it always was.

"You're going to wave that in front of me and tell me that I can't have any?"

"That was exactly what I told you," Ankh replied, shutting and securing the bridge access.

"It sucks owing that guy money," Red complained.

"Such is life. Lindy and Jay, we're going on the orbiting cruise liner in order to look for a party. Jay takes the lead because Floyd will be so cute that everyone will want to pet her. No one will notice us. We'll canvass the area and see if anyone knows anything."

Lindy put her foot down verbally. "I'm staying close to you, Magistrate. That is non-negotiable."

"Fine. I'm not going anywhere."

I'm cute! Floyd said all of a sudden, and everyone laughed except Tyler. After a few moments, the chuckles subsided. Jay vigorously rubbed the wombat's body, making the little girl giggle into their minds.

"We should have given him a chip," Red whispered urgently. "He's a liability without it."

Tyler eased into the open area.

"I know," Rivka replied, talking softly behind her hand. "You keep him out of harm's way."

"If anything happens, I'm going in heavy."

"I figured. Make sure Ankh keeps you up to speed. He'll be tracking us for the duration."

"And for the record, dudes won't care about Floyd. They'll only have eyes for the hot women. You aren't exactly going to be dressed like wallflowers." Red was serious, not doing his best to improve the team's situational awareness.

"That's what we're going for, but we'll keep our eyes out. If we have to deploy Floyd as part of our battle strategy, she's ready."

Floyd is ready to fight! the wombat declared.

Red stared like a stunned mullet. He couldn't imagine how Floyd could contribute if things got out of hand, but he knew that the Magistrate and Lindy could handle themselves as long as there weren't too many combatants. He shook his head.

"I don't want anyone to get hurt. Period. Bottom line. End of story."

Rivka winked at her bodyguard as the group disappeared into their quarters, returning fairly quickly after a complete change of clothes. Red found it hard not to stare.

Lindy stood on her toes to give Red a kiss. "We'll be fine. I'm afraid for the guys we want to talk to, but you know what they say. You have to break a few eggs to make an omelet or something like that. I'm not sure I've ever had a real egg."

"Not all they're cracked up to be," Rivka added. "We are looking for Callius Markmal. Everyone else is an hors d'oeuvre. I want the main course."

The look in Rivka's eye suggested that she would have it even if she had to tear the luxury ship apart.

"Try the soft sell first," Red suggested.

"I can't believe you think I would go in there like a bistok in a glass factory." Rivka put her hands on her hips after smoothing a fold on her slinky black dress.

"There is a history..." Red let the words hang in the air. Lindy nodded her agreement as she flexed her hands as if preparing herself for a fight. Jay continued to stroke the wombat's fur.

Rivka waved Reaper, the neutron pulse weapon, in the air and then tucked it into her clutch. "Shall we, ladies?"

Wheee! Floyd squealed.

Red's expression was grim as he started to gear up. "Just say the word, and I'm coming in."

The dentist looked appalled. "This is how you do it?" he asked.

The team nodded as one. "Pretty much," Rivka replied.

"I'm assuming that thing you stuffed in your purse is a weapon. You're dressed for a party but ready to beat people senseless?"

"Pretty much," Rivka repeated. "Stay on the ship, Doc. We'll be back." He continued to look aghast as the three women tiptoed through the ship in their high heels.

Lindy cycled the airlock, exposing the access tunnel beyond.

"Ladies, it's showtime. I need information, and this is where we're going to get it." Rivka said as she followed Lindy into the liner on their way to the executive level to find the reality star.

"You aren't allowed upstairs without an invitation," the bot said.

"Maybe you could bat your eyelashes at it?" Lindy suggested. Rivka looked over her shoulder at her bodyguard.

"There seems to be a flaw in our evil plan to get Callius to sign our breasts," Rivka replied. When Rivka turned back, the bot retreated.

"You may enter, but not the rodent of unusual size."

"She's a wombat, and her name is Floyd," Jay said, her head held high. "She's not a rodent!"

"The wombat cannot enter," the bot clarified.

Nooo! Floyd cried, and she started to fuss.

"We'll go back to the ship," Jay said sadly.

"We won't be long," Rivka replied in a cold and hard voice.

"Not long at all," Lindy reiterated.

Jay put Floyd on the deck and they walked slowly away.

Rivka tipped her head toward the door and took one step, and it opened without any manual intervention. The bot looked like it was part of the wall without lights or movement to show that it was active.

They headed up the stairs, Lindy staying one step back and on Rivka's left side. If the Magistrate drew her weapon, it would be with her right hand, which didn't interfere with Lindy's field of fire. She also had a weapon; not the compact neutron pulse device, but a hand blaster secreted in a ruffle on the train, which looked almost like a cape and flowed from the back of her dress. The Magistrate didn't know about it, but Red had refused to send her in unarmed. Lindy had agreed.

At the top of the steps, a large man filled the role of bouncer or the second last line of defense for the celebrity and his inner circle. The large man looked bored.

Lindy smirked at his size—smaller than Red, he was less intimidating. *I can take him,* she thought.

Rivka shook her head almost imperceptibly. She smiled broadly and waved. "Can you show us to Mister Markmal?"

"Security check. Hold your arms out." Rivka did as directed and he patted her down too thoroughly, copping a feel as he did so. He took her clutch from her hand and looked inside, quickly handing it back.

"Now you," he told Lindy.

"If you try to grab me like that, I'll break your face." Lindy glared at him as she put her arms out. Rivka grabbed his arm as he reached for Lindy.

"She has had some trauma. You don't need her hell all over you," Rivka warned while trying to interpret the thoughts going through his filthy mind. "Mister Markmal?"

He showed her exactly where he was, and that the celebrity was alone. Rivka checked the short corridor. Only two doors. "What's through that other door?"

"What?" the security guard asked. By then, Rivka had all she needed.

"We're alone," she said to Lindy. "Finish him."

Lindy's hand shot out at the speed of light, delivering a devastating throat punch. He bounced off the back wall and started to gag. She followed with a roundhouse to the side of the head and he went head over heels, rolling once before coming to a stop. He gurgled slightly but was still getting air.

"We'll throw him in there. It's a party room, but it's empty." They each grabbed an arm and dragged him to the door, opening it and throwing him inside. Rivka followed him in. "I judge you guilty of sexual misconduct. Your punishment for unwanted touching is that every other finger will be broken. Rivka quickly snapped the finger bones and left the man to his fate. She stopped before leaving. "And this is from me."

She kicked his knee and twisted. The kneecap shattered under the blow. "Asshole."

Across the hallway was the door behind which they'd find their quarry.

Rivka straightened her dress, and Lindy pulled her pistol and held it behind her back. The Magistrate knocked lightly. "Mister Markmal?" she called and threw the handle to open the door.

It was pitch-black inside.

"Follow the sound of my voice," he said in a breathy whisper.

"Lights!" Rivka stated, and the room lights came on, showing a naked Callius Markmal on his bed.

"Lights!" he shouted, and darkness returned. Rivka had the misfortune of having Markmal's form burned into her retinas.

"Fine," she said, allowing her low-light vision ability to guide her. "Hold the door open, please."

Lindy remained in the hallway, watching for any surprises while Rivka went inside.

"You'll need to close the door if you want to climb in

with me. I'm not opposed to a threesome, but I *am* opposed to doing it in front of an open door."

"There will be no threesome, twosome, or any-some. I need information, and you're the only one who has it." Rivka jumped to the side of the bed, grabbed his arm, and dragged him halfway to the floor to keep him off-balance.

He started to complain, but it was too late. Rivka was in charge.

"Why are you kidnapping young women and selling them into slavery?"

"What?" His mind was as confused as his question suggested.

"What do you know of Seequa Holmes?"

"Who?" More confusion. Images of women flashed through his mind—too many for Rivka to make any sense of. None of the images were of the woman she'd discovered in a Corran cell.

"Who handles the women for you, and where is he?"

"Why do you want her?"

"Finally we're getting somewhere." Rivka retreated into her mind and activated her comm chip. *Ankh, get me everything you can on a Candi Matz. I need to know where she is right now.*

She has boarded a long-range shuttle and is preparing to blast away from the liner, the Crenellian replied almost instantly.

Lock her down! Rivka requested.

The ship has launched and cut all digital ties with the cruise liner. They are attempting to make themselves a hole in space.

But you can still track them? Rivka had no doubt what the answer would be.

Of course.

We'll be home shortly. Prepare an intercept course, and we'll launch the second we get back.

"Why is Matz running?" Rivka demanded.

"She is?" the man asked, wondering where the intruder was getting her information.

"Do you know anything? Don't answer that. I already know you don't. You, sir, are an absolute pig, abhorrent in every way, but I don't see where you've broken any laws, as surprising as that is. Appalling, actually. Don't cross me ever again, and if I find out you've been feeding your Candi Matz victims, I'll come down on you like a battleship landing on a shantytown."

"Who the hell are you?" Callius shouted, finding his man-voice.

"I'm Magistrate Rivka Anoa, now shut up," Rivka told him, and twisted his arm until he stopped resisting.

"We need to get going, Magistrate," Lindy warned. With one arm, Rivka lifted the struggling celebrity and tossed him onto his bed.

"I better not ever see you again." Rivka pointed a finger-gun at him to make it clear what the consequences might be.

Once free of the Magistrate's grip, Callius laced his hands behind his head as he leaned back against the pillows. "I'm everywhere, baby, and you'll regret that you missed this. Lights!"

Rivka was already walking from the room when he put his nakedness on full display. She didn't turn back.

CHAPTER EIGHT

Rivka hammered the big red button as soon as she was through the airlock. A faint clunk from the other side reported the release of the access tube, and *Peacekeeper* started to move away. It accelerated steadily until Chaz reported the Gate drive was fully charged.

"We can follow her, or we can disable her ship and seize her," Ankh offered from the bridge.

"We don't need to follow her. I can take what I need from her mind." Rivka walked lightly toward her quarters but stopped when she saw the look on Tyler's face.

"Do you look into my mind?" he asked.

Rivka deflated. "I don't. Sometimes I can force it to stop. It's a gift and a curse. It haunts me, because no one should see into anyone else's mind."

"But you can look into suspects' minds?"

"That's different. I only do it when I have probable cause."

"As defined by you," the dentist countered.

"That is part of the burden. I don't have to defend it

before I use it, but I sure as hell have to defend it afterward, all the way to the High Chancellor. I include everyone I've interrogated in my reports, even those who are clear. Chaz keeps a good record."

"Who watches the watchers?" Tyler remarked.

"Everyone needs a watcher. No one should be able to hear others' thoughts, but these things are as they are. I have to maintain my moral compass at all times so I can look people like you in the eye and not be ashamed."

"People like me?"

"Innocents. Those I am sworn to protect. I can only stop criminals from breaking the law *again*. I stress the word again because they have to break the law before I can do anything. Just like that sock-slapping toad, Callius Markmal."

Jay bumped against the dentist. "You ever been in love, Doc?"

He shook his head. Floyd rubbed against his leg while Hamlet watched from nearby. The cat vaulted to the table, keeping his eyes on Tyler while he groomed himself.

"I think it would be like that," Jay continued. "Complete trust. No doubts. And for the record, I haven't been, either. Still waiting on Miss Right."

"I thought that you and Lauton had a little thing going." Rivka smiled.

"My boss forever keeps me in space, so there's no nurturing to see if the little thing can grow." She assumed her power stance, feet shoulder-width apart and fists on her hips.

"Well, there is that. Your boss is kind and generous and responsible for finding and punishing criminals in an entire galaxy. Consequently, we should have more potlucks."

"What?" the dentist asked. "What's a potluck?"

"Everyone brings a dish, and we all sit around and eat," Rivka replied.

"But you have a food processor and someone who can make it do stuff I never thought possible." He nodded toward the bridge.

"A potluck isn't about the food. It's about the company."

"Then why bring food?" he wondered.

"Because it's about the food," Jay replied.

"Not about the food," Rivka countered.

"Gate drive is active. Our goal is to appear in front of the target ship, which should be unarmed. I will request they heave to and prepare to be boarded, and I'll target the engines with minimal power plasma bursts should they not immediately comply," Chaz reported.

"And when it turns out they are armed and shielded?"

"Railgun capacitors are charged, and our shields are up."

"Do not destroy them, Chaz. I need to know what she knows. There's more than just her."

"I shall do my best. Erasmus is handling the targeting, so we should be able to disable the vessel without issue."

"I'm going to change first. Full combat gear. If they force us to take their ship, I want it to happen quickly."

"Take your seats, people," Rivka ordered, twirling her finger in the air. "Chaz. Gate us out, and let's go collect our runner."

A few moments later, the ship's AI reported that the Gate had formed and *Peacekeeper* was headed through. Shortly after that, the ship bucked and rocked before returning fire.

Rivka remained belted into her seat in the rec room. Red glanced at her. "Guess she wasn't unarmed."

"You're a master of understatement," Rivka called back.

The ship stopped juking and firing a short while later. Erasmus' voice came over the speakers. "The target ship has been disabled, but it is leaking atmosphere. You'll need to hurry to salvage what remains of the five life forms."

Red was first on his feet, followed by Lindy and Rivka. Jay bolted after Floyd, who fled after the first shot. The dentist remained in his seat.

Rivka tossed him the weight bar. "In case anyone gets past us, you'll need to protect the ship. Don't let anyone on board who's not us."

Red ran for the main hatch. The light turned green to confirm that they had a seal with the other ship and Red hit the button. He hoisted his railgun, ready to run into the breach. Lindy stayed close to Rivka.

"Don't fire unless you have no choice," Red cautioned. "We can't be punching holes in our ride."

"I couldn't agree more. Erasmus, are they conscious or injured?" Rivka asked.

"I suspect three are unconscious, and all five are injured."

Red nodded and held up two fingers to represent the

two possible active enemies. When the hatch popped open, he ducked his head in and quickly pulled back. "Clear," he announced, and ran into the tunnel. Rivka stayed behind him, using his body as a shield, just like he wanted. Lindy was right behind her.

They didn't see Tyler take up his position where he could peek around the corner of the hatch to watch for someone trying to infiltrate the Magistrate's ship. The bar rested on his shoulder, both hands gripped tightly around the end in case he needed to swing it. His heart pounded in his chest as the three disappeared into the small ship.

Red turned left at the opening and immediately took laser fire. Rivka pulled up short at the smell of burnt flesh. Red dove and rolled behind a cabinet, pulled out a stun grenade, waved it in the air, and then tossed it. Rivka and Lindy covered their ears and ducked away. Red did the same. Before the concussive blast finished reverberating through the long-distance shuttle's hull, Red was up and running.

In three steps, he found himself looming over two moaning crewmen with blood trickling from their ears and noses. He ripped the weapons out of their hands and looked for the other three , who turned out to be up front and out cold.

"Clear!" Red yelled over his shoulder, and Lindy and Rivka hurried in. The bodyguards zip-tied the conscious crewmen and searched the unconscious people for weapons. The injuries weren't life-threatening.

"This one," Rivka said, pointing to a woman in the cockpit. Lindy sat her up and rolled the unconscious form onto her shoulder before standing up.

"What do we do with these others?" Red asked.

"I should probably *talk* to all of them, but let's put that one on the *Peacekeeper*. Make sure she's bound before you do anything. If she's a slave trader, she'll come out of it spitting vinegar, and we just can't have that, now can we?" Rivka studied the woman for a moment before slapping a bandage on an ugly cut that dripped blood down her arm.

I haven't seen into her mind yet, but I've already judged her guilty. Leaving the luxury cruiser and heading into space may have been a terrible coincidence, but it was not *a crime,* Rivka counseled herself. *Innocent until proven guilty.*

Lindy ambled toward the airlock and Red looked at the four remaining in his charge. Rivka took one of the unconscious for first aid, and Red took the other. They quickly bandaged and patched them up, but they needed better care than the Magistrate and her crew could provide. She made a face, and Red shook his head.

"I guess we're loading them all up and heading back to the house?" Red suggested.

"Back to *our* house," Rivka clarified.

They carried the injured one at a time into *Peacekeeper* before throwing the last two over their shoulders and lugging them through the airlock.

"Ankh! Secure that ship, drop an encrypted beacon on it, and disconnect us. Next stop, Border Station 7."

"You don't have to yell," Ankh said over the speakers. The hatch to the bridge remained closed.

Doctor Toofakre was fully engaged with the medical kit, suturing the cut on Candi's arm. She also wore a mask through which supplemental oxygen flowed. At the same time, he was giving instructions to Jay on what to do with her patient. He stopped what he was doing to examine the third injured crewmember, then ordered Red and Rivka to hold the lower leg while he yanked it into position, allowing the tibia to realign itself.

"Put a splint on that," he directed. Rivka didn't hesitate. She had looked at the medical kit before but hadn't registered how robust it was. The case held enough bits, pieces, pads, pills, and tools to perform minor surgery or patch up a crew that was on the wrong end of a space battle.

While Rivka put the splint in place, Red pulled a hidden weapon from a leg sheath. He checked the other four and found similar blades. Two of the crew had small stun guns. One had a single-shot slug thrower.

"Now we're getting somewhere," Rivka noted. "Goes from being a strange coincidence regarding the timing of their departure to a band of armed criminals running from the law."

"Any of this stuff criminal?" Lindy asked.

"Not really; misdemeanors depending on licensing and planetary law. The crime is that they didn't stop when ordered by competent authority—well, and fired on us— but that's a slushy part of the law. Can I show probable cause regarding the need for search and seizure? Their privacy is sacrosanct unless they surrendered it through the commission of a crime or the appearance of the commission of a crime."

"Do you always talk like that?" Tyler wondered.

"It's what I'm good at," Rivka replied. "Like you're good with the medical stuff. I thought you were a dentist?"

"Dentists get trained in all kinds of stuff. We're the galactic jacks of all trades."

"Because no one has bad teeth anymore?" Red suggested with a hearty laugh.

"It's exactly like that, except completely different," Tyler shot back, smiling at the big man. Red was keeping a firm grip on the unconscious patients in case they woke up.

Peacekeeper shifted as Chaz adjusted the heading toward clear space in order to establish a Gate. The long-range shuttle continued to stream a small amount of debris.

"Gate formed. Next stop, Federation Border Station 7. Station Security will meet us in the hangar," Chaz reported.

"Do we risk waking them up before then?" Rivka asked, looking at the dentist.

"I wouldn't. When someone is unconscious, it's because the body is healing itself. It shuts down non-essential systems, to put it in spaceship vernacular. After a certain amount of time, we can revisit that, but they've only been out for fifteen minutes. Their bodies have undergone extreme trauma."

"They shouldn't have run from us. That's a great way to die tired." Red looked proud of himself.

"Although I don't agree with the conclusion, I do agree with the premise. They shouldn't have run." Rivka rubbed her chin as she thought through her options. "Segregate them when they come to. It won't take long to determine what they were up to."

"I don't like her." Lindy loomed over Candi Matz and glared.

One of the shuttle's crew groaned. Rivka hurried to him and took his arm to help him sit up. He was one who had been stunned.

"Why did you shoot at us?" she asked.

His mind was a swirl of mixed emotions and raging colors as he fought his way back to consciousness. Failure. Fear. Pain.

"What is your connection to the slave trade?" Rivka pressed.

His mind started to clear. An image of a sedated Seequa Holmes jumped into his mind. They had used that very shuttle to transport her. One of the injured was there against her will. They had unbound her when the fight with *Peacekeeper* started.

Rivka pointed. "Free that one. She's a victim." Jay and Red hurried to help the woman and move her to one of the recliners before covering her with a blanket to make her more comfortable. The Magistrate frowned. "Ankh," she said in a low voice, "where was the shuttle headed? It wasn't on a course for Corran, was it?"

"It was not," Erasmus answered for Ankh. "From the shuttle's profile and flight logs, it was headed for Fenek Eudoxius."

"Never heard of it." Rivka moved to Candi's side. "Doc, I need you to bring her out of it."

"I can't, not with the equipment you have here." He held his hands up in surrender. The look on his face was all Rivka needed to know that he was telling the truth. She tucked her hands into her pockets. "Get all of them to medical and let the healing begin. I want to know more about this one when she comes to."

Rivka stood by the side of the recliner.

"What happened to you?" Rivka whispered as she held the young woman's hand, her face still contorted by the pain of her injuries. "Can't you give her something?"

"Administer pain reliever while someone is unconscious? No. I won't do it."

"Not asking you to," Rivka replied, waving the dentist off. "I just wondered."

"Is every mission like this, with people getting hurt?" he asked.

"Every damn one, Doc! But it's usually us doing the bleeding, right after all the running." Red pounded the dentist on the back so hard, Tyler staggered and almost coughed out his tongue.

"Probably too often," the Magistrate admitted.

"We could use a sawbones." Red pointed with his chin toward Tyler.

Rivka pinched the bridge of her nose at the discomfort of being in the middle. She had no intention of bringing another person on board to be a member of the crew.

Floyd waddled into the area after having disappeared with the commotion and the emotion of combat. She sniffed Candi Matz, wrinkling her nose before moving to the next person. The groaner winced and tried to back away, but the zip ties held him tightly to a chair.

With a gentle bump, *Peacekeeper* landed in the hangar bay of their home port.

"Security is waiting outside the hatch along with Magistrate Grainger," Chaz reported.

"On it." Lindy hurried around the corner and down the short corridor. After she opened the hatch and extended the stairs, Grainger was first up. "Magistrate."

"Lindy. These barbarians aren't leading you astray, are they?"

The bodyguard shook her head, unsure of how she was supposed to answer.

"I didn't get an invitation to your wedding. I was *very* put out," Grainger quipped.

"We didn't get married."

"Good! Make sure I get an invite when you do. Red promised me that I'd get to walk him down the aisle."

Lindy's mouth fell open and she stared. Grainger stared back.

"The stuff that comes out of your mouth!" Rivka broke the stalemate. "No one is walking anyone down any aisle unless they are, but that's their choice, not yours. We'll be in All Guns Blazing sampling the reception meal."

"Do I get a say in this?" Lindy asked.

As one, the two Magistrates turned to her and said, "No."

"We have four unconscious, and one who just came to. He was in on the Seequa Holmes kidnapping and the seizure of that one in the recliner." Rivka pointed. "I think we have four traffickers and one victim, but we'll need to patch them up more than the triage approach to keep them alive. The doc did a bang-up job on our perps and the victim. I hate to admit it, but we could use a medical professional more often than not."

"In case a tooth gets knocked loose?" Grainger countered, looking pointedly at the dentist, who was covered in the blood of the injured. Tyler emotionlessly studied the Magistrate.

"He knows a lot more than that."

"Denied. Resubmit in thirty days for final denial." He

gave the dentist a thumbs-up. "This isn't a business you want to be in, Doc."

Rivka shrugged. "I had to ask. I guess we're stuck with using band-aids and whiskey from the med kit."

The Magistrates stopped at the entrance to the rec room. There were blood stains in too many places, two perps zip-tied to chairs, an unconscious woman on a recliner, and two out cold on the deck. Rivka pointed to one of them. "Candi Matz. She's Callius Markmal's chief of operations. I think she's running a slave ring, but I haven't had the chance to talk to her."

"Is that the reality star guy?" Grainger scowled. "What a nut-lick."

Lindy escorted four security officers and four medical technicians into the ship, and Rivka and Grainger stepped aside. It was suddenly so crowded that one couldn't turn around. Jay excused herself, grabbed Floyd, and disappeared into her cabin.

"This one is a victim. Take care of her, and set her up in medical. We need to talk to her. These two are detained for questioning, so patch them up and maintain twenty-four/seven security until we say otherwise. Those two go straight into holding cells." Rivka pointed appropriately as she spoke, and the security and medical staff took over.

"Good job, Doc," Grainger told the dentist.

"You can call me 'Tyler,'" he offered.

"You wanna go back out with these guys?" Grainger abruptly asked.

"Permanently?" Tyler Toofakre wasn't taken with the idea.

"No, I've already denied that, but I mean on this case?

See it through to the end."

"Do all cases have an end?"

"I'm willing to bet good money that this one will get resolved. Mostly." Grainger gestured as if making his closing arguments to a jury. "We won't catch all the traders, but if we can interdict some of the major suppliers and make it too dangerous for the rest, Corran may give up the last vestiges of the business and join the Federation. Dry up the market, and the galaxy's scum can move onto something else; maybe even swear off crime entirely." Grainger made to go.

"We can always hope," Rivka agreed.

"I'll have to think about it," Tyler replied, a frown darkening his features as he stared at the floor, lost in thought.

Rivka put her hand gently on his shoulder. "Buck up, Doc. It only gets easier from here."

"Really?" he asked, brightening.

Red started to laugh. The dentist scowled.

"We always hope it gets easier. Sometimes the dominos fall by themselves. Other times, we need to give them a gentle nudge." Rivka looked at Grainger, who kept his opinion to himself.

He hesitated before nodding slowly one time. "I'll be with the people in sickbay. You take the conscious ones. Keep your datapad close in case the broken perps wake up." He headed off the ship, reiterating his orders to the security guards on where to take those in custody.

"Suspects," Rivka clarified, although Grainger was long out of hearing range. She shrugged, checked that Red and Lindy were following, and joined the group heading for the holding cells.

CHAPTER NINE

Rivka crossed her arms and glared at the suspect across the cold steel of the metal table. He tried to project calm, but a bead of sweat on his forehead and a vein throbbing in his neck gave him away. Rivka could have grabbed him to find the truth, but that would have been limited. If she convinced him to come clean, then she could focus what she asked to determine if it was the truth or not.

"Why did you kidnap that woman?" She set the stage for all that would follow.

"I don't know what you're talking about." His defenses were up, but they were weak.

Rivka leaned forward and slapped the table when she dropped her hands. He jumped. "Do you want me to rip it from your mind? That would be a tad uncomfortable. You can just tell me, and then we can move forward like adults."

He tried to fold his arms, but his handcuffs stopped him. He looked annoyed at the unsavory bracelets.

"I tried the easy way, but I don't have time for any ridiculous thrust and parry." She stood while he snickered at the reference. She walked around behind him, and he shifted to keep her in front of him. "Fine," she declared as she stomped her foot onto his hands and drove them into his groin. She grabbed his chin. "I asked why you kidnapped that woman."

Images flashed into her mind. Candi Matz directing the team. An event filled with willing women. Too much booze. The team descended and removed her. The others studiously avoided looking at the passed-out girl being carried away by Security. Business as usual, so no one is uncomfortable at a Callius Markmal party.

"Did Candi Matz direct the abduction?" More images. The team practiced the delivery of the spiked drink and the choreography of the selection and pickup.

"How much do you get paid for each person you deliver?"

A computer screen showing a stack of credits. The image didn't show a number, but if it had, it would have been a big one.

"Where were you going, and who were you to meet?" Nothing. He didn't know.

"How were you going to transfer your victim?"

He assumed they were going to physically hand her to someone else and walk away. He didn't know that part either.

"It must suck to be a lackey. You think you have plausible deniability because you weren't in on the rest of the plan?" Rivka asked, moving back to her side of the table.

He stared at her without speaking.

"I am Magistrate Rivka Anoa, and under the authority granted me under Federation Law, you are hereby sentenced to death for your role in the trafficking of Federation citizens. Do you have any last words before I carry out the sentence?"

He started to look around frantically. "What?" he blurted. "That's it? But I was just a hired hand trying to make a buck. I had nothing to do with the trade. I was just following orders."

"Just following orders," Rivka repeated as she began to pace, never taking her eyes off the man who was now sweating profusely and vibrating with fear. "What if you had said no? What if the others had said no? Then there would have been no crime. But you were a witting ally, not just a lackey. You were helping make the slave trade possible, and you did it with the full understanding that you would be well paid. My regret is that I didn't catch you and your fellow scumbags earlier, but I have you all now. You have willfully committed a capital crime, but I'm going to modify your sentence because death is too good for the likes of you. Your punishment is that you'll serve the rest of your life on Jhiordaan. You will learn what it's like to be a slave, in that you will never take another breath of free air. Don't you worry—you won't be going alone. The other three will be joining you shortly for your transfer."

Rivka turned to one of the two guards in the room and stabbed a thumb over her shoulder. "Get that one ready for transfer to the prison colony, and hold three more seats. They'll be filled with puckered buttholes shortly."

The guard snickered. Red nodded to the woman as he and Lindy followed the Magistrate out of the room.

"Do you need to talk to the other jailbird?" Red asked.

"I don't think so. I already saw what he had to say, so I

can skip him. Let's go to the med lab and see how Candi is doing. The evidence is overwhelming, so we'll proceed under the firm belief that not only is she guilty of trafficking, but she's the ring leader. I want to know her contact at the destination, because as of the moment we stopped their shuttle, she became a pawn in the big game. She's not a player. I want to topple the king and queen. They're still out there." Rivka pointed in the general direction of the closest external station bulkhead.

"I want to see you topple them," Lindy confirmed.

"Yeah. Fuck those guys," Red agreed.

"Hating on the kingpins?" the Magistrate asked.

"I have a history with those types. Most are pricks. Rarely do you find ones like the High Chancellor or Nathan Lowell, or even Lance Reynolds. Those guys are solid leaders of empires, but they don't climb over the backs of the downtrodden to get there."

"Too true, my friend," Rivka replied. Lindy nodded vigorously. "Next stop, sickbay."

"There's nothing you can do for her?" Grainger asked the technician.

"It wasn't her injuries. There's something else. It's as if she's trying to die." The technician looked at the numbers and lines on a screen next to the bed and shook her head.

The door slid open. Rivka, Red, and Lindy walked in and made a beeline for Grainger.

"I'm sorry," the technician said before moving to another patient.

"Sorry for what?" Rivka asked. She groaned when she saw who it was. "Candi Matz. You're a bastard."

"She has no intention of living," Grainger said. "What did you get from the ones downstairs?"

"They did it because they were paid well, and it was the boss who asked them to do it. But they had no idea where they were going or who they were meeting with. That information is locked up inside there." Rivka pointed to the woman whose face was obscured by a mask.

Rivka touched her arm and asked, "Where were you going and who were you meeting?" She studied the woman's face. "Nothing there."

A steady tone sounded as Candi Matz flatlined.

"I guess her sentence was death," Grainger remarked before tapping his pad to request a full autopsy.

"You think she suicided?"

"I do. We'll see if the autopsy confirms it, but I expect it to be inconclusive." The medical technician stepped in to shut off the alarm and pull the sheet over the woman's face before returning to her previous patient.

"Ankh said the ship was headed for Fenek Eudoxius. I wanted the perps to confirm it, though, and tell me who they were going to meet."

"That last part is key."

"And I think Candi died to protect the information. Maybe she knew she was just a pawn. That suggests they had something on her." Rivka relaxed as she started to pity the woman.

"Like her family?"

Rivka removed her datapad from the inside pocket of her Magistrate jacket. "Ankh, can you check on Candi

Matz's family, like a sister, a mother, children, people who could be used to coerce her to join the traffickers. Find me everything you can, especially their whereabouts. She was paid well. They all were, but in her case, there has to be something else."

"Erasmus will look into it. I'm busy at the moment." Ankh cut the connection.

Grainger's eyebrows went up before he started to laugh. "Genius comes at a price, doesn't it?"

"I don't care if it's Ankh or Erasmus who gets me the information as long as I get it. Our friendly Crenellian might have some rough edges, but he's saved our lives more than once, and I *know* that he will again. I'm happy to have him on the team." She waved Grainger off as if chasing away a fly. Rivka turned to the technician and called, "How is our young lady?"

"We're flushing her system to clear out the drugs. It was a heavy mix that we haven't seen before: a narcotic and sedative combined. Nasty stuff. I wouldn't be surprised if half the people given this cocktail didn't survive."

Rivka clenched her jaw and put her hands in her pockets. She stood as rigid as a bulkhead frame. There would be no *testimony* that day.

"Lunch?" Lindy asked.

"Sounds great!" Red replied.

Lindy rolled her eyes. "I wasn't talking to you." The two clasped hands.

"Not yet," Rivka said, relaxing through a forced smile. "Let's see if this one knows anything. Can you wake him up, please?"

"That is not advised," the technician answered with a

passive construct, avoiding any responsibility for the judgment.

"Under my authority as a Federation Magistrate, wake him up." Rivka's tone suggested there could be no objection.

The technician prepared a drug to deliver through the IV. "This is not advised," the woman repeated. Rivka impatiently stabbed a finger at the tube disappearing under the tape on the perp's arm. The technician relented and administered the medicine, then made to remove the mask through which precious oxygen flowed.

"Leave it," Rivka directed.

"But you won't be able to understand his answers."

"But I will." Rivka's expression softened. "I understand that you are only trying to do your job and help those who can't help themselves. I'm doing the same thing. That woman who died, and this person? They have been kidnapping people like her," she pointed to the unconscious young woman, "and selling them as slaves. I need this information so we can stop the next expected sale and work our way up the ladder until we have the one in charge. I don't care if this scumbag dies, but I don't want it to happen before I can ask him a few questions."

"I think your capital punishment attitude is deplorable!" the medical technician shot back. Grainger raised a questioning eyebrow.

"His punishment will be Jhiordaan. Your efforts to save his life will not have been in vain." Rivka smiled, close-lipped, but the woman harrumphed and moved away.

Red swelled as he stretched to his full height and scowled at the medical technician.

The Magistrate started to say something to him, but a groan from the bed drew their attention. Rivka immediately gripped his arm and looked into his wild and pain-filled eyes.

"Who were you delivering the woman to?" she blurted. Scattered images splattered with the emotion of Rivka's attack on the long-range shuttle danced through his mind.

"WHO?" Rivka shouted, and an alien face appeared. Rivka embraced it and memorized it. A trigger. He mentally pulled it and started to quickly fade. An alarm sounded on the monitor next to the bed. Rivka let the man's arm drop.

"They have a kill switch in their brains," Rivka said softly. "It releases a small but lethal dose."

"Did you get what you needed?"

"Yes. I need to link my comm with Ankh and concentrate. I think we can get a picture, and I hope that leads to a name."

Grainger approached the medical technician, whose eyes glistened with tears that refused to fall. "They both suicided to prevent giving up the information. That is the level of criminal that we're dealing with. You did everything you could, but their lives were out of all our hands. Someone out there is pulling the strings." Grainger said softly, finishing with a nod toward the greater universe. Out there. Where the real criminal waited.

"Let us know the instant she's awake, please," Grainger pleaded with the technician. She nodded stiffly.

Rivka sat down and closed her eyes, then held her head to focus on taking the image from her mind's eye and sending it over the comm link to Ankh and Erasmus.

Time dragged on as she concentrated to the exclusion of everything happening around her.

Ankh's small voice projected into her mind. *I have it.*

Rivka leaned back and blinked her eyes open. "Who's ready for lunch?"

CHAPTER TEN

Jay chased Floyd while those working on the hangar deck stopped to watch. The wombat was surprisingly fast when she wanted to be, especially during the game of Keep-away. Jay laughed like the teenager she was. Rivka, Lindy, and Red stopped to watch too, enjoying the simple fun of the pursuit. Floyd giggled into their minds even as she squealed out loud.

She raced between Jay's legs, tripping the young woman whose flaming red hair sparkled against the darkness of space beyond the viewport.

Rivka waved when Jay spotted her, then jumped to her feet and ran in a tight circle after the wombat. She tapped Floyd's head as she passed. The creature turned and chased Jay, who demonstrated the ability to zig-zag and sprint, jump, and dodge. She slowed enough to let Floyd catch her. The two strolled casually back, both breathing heavily as they joined the Magistrate and her bodyguards.

"I'm glad to see you happy, Jay." Rivka remembered the

juvenile delinquent who had given her the finger. She almost regretted dislocating said finger.

Almost.

"Where to next, boss?" Jay picked up the wombat, who snuggled into her arms and instantly fell asleep.

"I wish I could do that," Red grumbled.

"You can." Lindy shook her head.

"No way. That was two seconds!"

"Your personal best is seven seconds from speaking to snoring. I don't see the difference."

"Sounds trivial when you put it like that."

"I'm envious of both of you."

"No kidding," Rivka agreed. "Next stop for the *Peacekeeper* Express is Fenek Eudoxius. Grainger is going to stay with the victim so we can get going. The first stop is to pick up that long-range shuttle. We need it. I have a plan."

"You don't have to tell me. I already know what it is..." Jay let the words drift as she turned toward the corvette, stroking Floyd's ear with one finger while cradling her like a baby. The others followed, leaving the hatch open after they boarded.

"Waiting for Tyler. He'll be here shortly," Rivka explained. She tapped on the hatch to the bridge until it opened. Ankh was in the captain's chair, which was now heavily modified and sporting a holo grid that surrounded the Crenellian. "I should have never let him move to the bridge."

"Hush," Ankh said as he tapped, swiped, and danced within the complex grid. Rivka sucked in a breath through flared nostrils. Red stood back, wondering if there would be fireworks.

The holo grid dissolved and Ankh cracked his knuckles. "At your service, Magistrate," he said emotionlessly.

She had to ask. "What were you working on?"

"Refining the Gate drive miniaturization. Ted and I have just sent our upgraded design to R2D2 for testing. With at least an EI, even a Pod would be able to carry and use a functional Gate drive."

"That's all? I thought you were working on something important," Rivka deadpanned. She waited, but her jibe didn't get a rise out of the Crenellian. "What did you find out about Candi Matz's family?"

Erasmus answered using the overhead speakers. "Her parents passed away, and she has no siblings."

"Well, now. That drives a dagger into the heart of my theory." Rivka's mind stepped back to square one. She crossed her arms and stared at one of the few empty spots on the wall.

"However, she corresponds regularly with another female her age, who is located on Fenek Eudoxius."

Rivka smiled. "Bingo."

"Hi, honey! I'm home," Dr. Toofakre called from the hallway.

"Punch the button," Red told him. "It's time to go. We got perps to roust."

Chaz chimed in. "Preparing to depart the station. Please take your places."

"I'll need you to stop by that long-range shuttle first; see if we can salvage it. Best possible speed, Chaz," Rivka ordered.

Ankh made a shooing motion with his small arm.

"When this case is concluded, I'm taking my bridge back."

Ankh stared at her without blinking. She stared back. They remained like that until Rivka's eyes started to burn. Red & Lindy left them to it. Hamlet made his way onto the bridge, jumped into the captain's chair, and started to make himself comfortable. Ankh tried to push him away, but the cat avoided his hands.

"Fine," Ankh said noncommittally. He broke eye contact and used both hands to shove Hamlet off the chair. With a hiss and swipe of a paw, three parallel red lines appeared on the Crenellian's arm, a drip of blood trailing from each. "I don't like your cat."

"He's not *my* cat. He comes with the ship." Rivka bit her lip to keep from laughing as she walked out.

"The atmosphere has vented and the environmental controls are offline," Chaz reported.

"Which means it's cold and without air," Red remarked.

Ankh stood in his shipsuit, helmet pulled over his head and inflated, wearing a coat and supplemental gloves. The others only wore their shipsuits, their bodies teeming with nanocytes to keep them warm until the umbilical from *Peacekeeper* pumped enough air and heat into the shuttle to make it comfortable.

Or at least, *less* lethal.

"I can direct you to do the work or a maintenance bot," Ankh said.

"You're going. Time is of the essence if we're going to masquerade as Candi and her goons," Rivka explained.

"It won't work. They have met her before. Who else would have put the suicide solution in their brains?"

"I don't need to fool them when we're face to face," Rivka argued. "All we have to do is create enough doubt to get in the door."

"I cast doubt on your effort to create doubt," Ankh said before going to work beneath the control panel in the cockpit while two maintenance bots entered the crawl-space to the engine compartment. Erasmus guided their efforts while Chaz pumped heated air through the tube connecting the two ships in the middle of interstellar space. A series of clunks reported the efforts of a bot working on the outer hull.

The lights flickered but remained off.

Using flashlights, Red, Lindy, and Rivka searched the small ship for any clues that might have been inadvertently left behind by the crew. The small cabins with three-high bunk beds were mostly empty.

The lights flickered and came to life.

Then the life support system started recycling the air and heating the shuttle to a more suitable temperature.

You can turn off the heat, Chaz, but be ready to turn it back on. I think Ankh is duct-taping this ship back together, Rivka said.

I heard that, Ankh replied over their internal communication system. *When I'm finished, this ship will be ready to continue its journey to Fenek Eudoxius.*

"When will that be?" Rivka was taken aback. When they arrived at the long-range shuttle less than an hour earlier, her initial impression was the ship was nothing more than scrap. *Peacekeeper*'s weapons had been well aimed, but the shuttle was small, and the damage appeared to be extensive.

Cosmetic, Ankh informed them as if reading her mind. *That should be it. One last series of welds on the hull and we're done.*

Rivka wanted to ask once more when that would be, but Ankh brushed past on his way back to *Peacekeeper*.

"Are you done?" she asked. Red blocked his way. The Crenellian tilted his head back to look up at the big man until it seemed like he would fall over. Red crossed his arms and pointed with his chin toward the Magistrate.

Instead, Ankh looked at the access hatch in the deck, which popped open. Two maintenance bots climbed out, and a final heavy clunk heard through the hull signaled that the bot working outside the ship had detached. The rest of the team removed their hoods and secured their ship suits from full containment.

"Now we are finished."

"You are a miracle worker, Ankh."

Rivka's beaming smile and platitudes were lost on the alien. "I would say that this work was below my paygrade, but I recognize that we all do the tasks necessary to complete the mission—"

"Case," Rivka corrected, but Ankh didn't notice.

"I like working with Ted, Erasmus, and Plato in the development of new technologies. But I also like putting criminals away. There is a certain order in the galaxy that must be maintained. That helps free us to explore new possibilities using only our minds because we are safe. I have accepted my mission to help you in expectation of the day when the galaxy is secure enough that all of us can be at peace and free to enjoy what we choose to do."

"Damn, little man," Red said. "If we can accomplish that, I'll be out of a job."

"*We'll* be out of jobs," Lindy added. "And then we can take our honeymoon and be like a real couple. What will *you* do, Magistrate?"

"I... I don't know," Rivka stuttered. "Maybe work on AGB franchises to bring them to all corners of the galaxy."

"The galaxy is elliptical in shape," Ankh stated matter-of-factly.

"Of course it is." Rivka looked past Red. "It's time, people! I need you two," Rivka pointed at Red and Lindy, "and Jay and Tyler to go with me on the shuttle. Ankh, you follow in the *Peacekeeper*."

Ankh nodded briefly and returned to the corvette. Jay and the dentist worked their way through the umbilical and stepped aboard. Tyler looked uncomfortable, and Jay carried Floyd.

"We can't bring Floyd." Rivka put her foot down.

Noooo! I small, Floyd tried to explain.

"It's not your size. It's the danger. I would put you in danger, in addition to jeopardizing the mission. You need to watch over Ankh and Hamlet. We'll be back together soon enough."

Floyd started to cry. Jay blinked as well, hugging the wombat tightly as she returned to their ship and put Floyd in the passageway. They both disappeared.

"Ankh, we may have to take a shortcut. If we Gate most of the way there, can we make up the lost time?"

"I will calculate an appropriate entry point that will put you right on schedule, less than a day out from Fenek."

"Late would be bad." Rivka nodded and headed for the cockpit. She took the pilot's seat and started mashing buttons to familiarize herself with the system.

"I'll be able to fly the boat for you," Chaz offered, speaking to her from a speaker linked into the main control panel.

"Hey, Chaz! Look at you, right in the middle of my pilot's station."

"Have you ever flown a spaceship before, Magistrate?"

Rivka leaned back. "I watch you do it all the time. Looks easy."

"I assure you it is not. May I request that you let me handle it?"

"You know, so you don't crash and kill us all?" Red interjected.

"Why do you have to be so hurtful? I mean, all of you!" Rivka shook her head and chuckled.

"Just the facts, ma'am," Red grumbled before retiring to the main cabin.

"Go ahead, Chaz. It's all you. Be the ship. What's this ship's name, anyway?"

"It has only its designation, which is LRS-4169."

"Sixty-nine!" Red called from somewhere out of sight. It was immediately followed by the sound of an arm getting punched, which was followed by a grunt of pain.

The airlock cycled, and *Peacekeeper* detached. Rivka could still hear Floyd's cries in her mind.

"What do we call her?" Rivka asked the team. She left

the bridge because Chaz had things well in hand, flying both ships in tandem.

"Gate forming," Chaz reported. "We will arrive at the edge of the gravity well a full day's travel from Fenek Eudoxius."

"Didn't we go through this with *Peacekeeper*?" Red asked.

The Magistrate smirked at the memory. It had taken a while to name her corvette. It had taken time to name their weapons.

Dr. Toofakre looked uncomfortable.

"What do you think, Doc?" Rivka asked.

"I think I have no idea what I'm doing. What will happen when we land? What happens if they're violent? Our cover is pretty thin."

"This is a crime ring, and those do have a tendency to be extremely violent when protecting their assets. However, we generally bring a great deal of pain, and our intent is to make a surgically precise extraction of the cancer that is the ringleader. Tomorrow this may all be over. Our perp could be in custody or dead, and their minions running for their lives. Sometimes it only takes one innocuous piece of information to break an organization's back."

"*Spinal Tap*," Tyler replied.

The Magistrate held her hands up and shook her head. Jay looked lost but was taking more interest in the conversation now that they could no longer hear the wombat.

"Name of the ship. *Spinal Tap*. I think it used to be a band, too."

Lindy was first to agree. "I like it."

"I'm good with it." Rivka gave two thumbs-up. "And this is us, which means that the ship probably won't make it to the end, so a temporary name could be its forever name."

"Our track record would suggest you are correct," Red noted, making his voice sound mechanical as if he were a computer delivering a simple report of the weather. Lindy started to laugh.

The dentist strolled among the group with his hands clasped behind his back. He looked from one face to another as he went back and forth.

"Danger," he started, but was slow to continue. "You people seem to laugh at danger, but in a way that suggests you are not afraid. That the pain *you* bring is much greater than what the criminals have at their command. It makes me want to pity them, but I know better. They are scumbags, and the universe is better off without them."

Tyler continued to pace. The rest of the team waited.

"*Peacekeeper* is remaining behind until a suitable separation has been established between them and the long-range shuttle," Chaz reported.

"*Spinal Tap*," the team said together.

"*Spinal Tap* it is," Chaz confirmed.

Dr. Toofakre continued, "Is it that hard to believe that people would be so committed to making the galaxy a safer place that they would be willing to risk it all like you folks do? You get no personal enrichment from it. At least I get paid after treating a patient."

"We have a yacht that the team has acquired," Red admitted.

"Confiscated," Rivka clarified.

"What did you have to do to get that?"

"Fight in a civil war," Lindy said first.

"But we were in the middle, fighting both sides at the same time," Jay explained.

"And then we were shot and burned by the tree guy," Red offered.

"Did we get shot during that one?" Rivka wondered.

"We got the holy hell beat out of us."

"I remember that part."

"We saw the mayor. That deserves a pain-and-suffering bonus."

"Those were grim days." The team chuckled together.

"'Seeing the mayor?'" Tyler asked.

Red made the twig and berries motion with his hands.

The dentist blanched. "I see." He gathered his wits. "I am thankful that there are people like you looking out for people like me. I won't take my peace and security for granted."

"We have a convert! Don't break the law. You don't want to see us beating your door down at oh too-early thirty," Red told him.

"I have no intention of breaking the law. Once word of your actions reaches the underworld, it should have a chilling effect on crime, I would think."

"Unfortunately, that's not how it works. All it does is increases the prices on our heads. We can't advertise what we do. Perps thinking they're safe is our best defense. Anything else and the scumbags are loaded for gorons, ready to blast the next person through their door."

"It's a shit show, Doc," Red clarified.

"I understand," the dentist said, shaking his head at Red's description.

"Study up!" Rivka commanded. "Erasmus has uploaded the planet's information file to your datapads. Study it and learn it. I'll be working the lines to set up a meeting with our as-yet-unknown contact."

"I'll be the vic," Lindy offered.

"Ain't gonna work," Rivka replied.

"Me?" Jay said meekly.

"You're the youngest and the cutest, so you're perfect slave material. Unfortunately. We won't let you out of our sight, and if it becomes necessary, run for your life. No one can catch you."

CHAPTER ELEVEN

"She's awake," Grainger declared from the big screen. The others listened in, since the rec room was a communal space. Rivka missed being able to have private conversations on the bridge.

I need a bigger ship, she complained in the landscape of her mind. Still, *Spinal Tap* made *Peacekeeper* seem luxurious. They had docked again after arrival in the system to attend to some details before going down to Fenek Eudoxius, although they had not originally planned to. Too bad Floyd would be upset—again—when they left—again.

"I wish you were here. She is mostly incoherent, unable to grasp where she is or how she got here. Maybe in a couple days, she'll settle down enough to have a conversation."

"Or maybe the drugs caused more grief than we thought. Psychotropics are bad news."

"We'll add that to the list of things we need to get to the bottom of. How and where? They must have their own chemist who dispenses meds for each targeted race. We're all the same, but we're all different."

"I already have it on my list of questions. *When* we catch these people, I know we'll have to launch an army of police to clean out the rats' nests scattered throughout the known worlds." Rivka slowly blew out her breath. "Did she give you anything at all?"

"We showed her pictures of her kidnappers, but she didn't remember any of them except for Candi Matz. And she asked if she could see her. It was a little disconcerting," Grainger admitted. "She doesn't understand that she was a victim, and I'm not sure how much I want to play into that. If she doesn't remember, I don't need to convince her. I'll leave that to the psychiatrists to unscrew."

"That may be the extent of what you need from her. Let her recover physically, then get her on the next express cruiser home."

"I was thinking the same thing. I'll turn her over to a security team to escort wherever she wants to go, except back to the cruise liner where she was kidnapped—although without Candi and her people, even that is probably safe."

"As long as she doesn't go see that pig Callius Markmal."

"Girls gone wild." Grainger repeated the social media siren's call. "She's free to do as she pleases."

"I know. People are responsible for their good decisions *and* their bad ones. He would be everyone's bad decision. Maybe people need a few of those in their lives, so they know where the boundaries are. Without evil, what would good look like? Without making some bad decisions, how can they tell if they're making good ones?"

"Too philosophical for my blood, Magistrate. I called to let you know that we're not getting anything from the vic, but she is awake and on her way to a full physical recovery, at least."

"Thanks, Leib..." Rivka caught herself before saying his name out loud in front of all the others. "Thanks. Leave it to us, Grainger. We're already in the traffic pattern for Fenek Eudoxius. Next stop, the planet's surface. Hopefully, the meeting with the locals will include someone who is expecting us to drop off a fire-haired slave girl."

"May your travels deliver a feast for your eyes and fill your soul beyond measure. Grainger out."

"Who's the philosopher now?" Rivka mumbled, chewing the inside of her lip. "Ankh, do you have anything for us?"

"I do," the alien replied. "I found the name Ch'ta'ka in the long-range shuttle's computer. I have set up a meeting. Details have been forwarded to your pad." He signed off.

The Magistrate removed her datapad from her jacket pocket and studied the information. "That does not instill confidence," she said to herself before locking up to address the group. "Red, Lindy, what is your armament plan?"

Red opened his mouth, but stopped and nodded to Lindy. If she could explain the plan, he would know they were both on the same page.

"The kidnappers had no body armor and limited weapons, so that's what we're going with—their slugthrowers. We will remain with you, keeping Jay between us. We want the doc to bring up the rear, staying out of sight and not speaking. You don't come across as a thug, Doc. Sorry. We're blessed in that department."

She waited for the snickers to stop before continuing.

"If there is an exchange, we take out any shooters on their side, preferably by disabling them. Jay will need to help us by using her speed to disarm them or ram them or whatever she needs to do, based on the situation. If they have shooters overlooking the area, Red and I will take them out. We'll leave the head honcho to you, Magistrate."

"What if we're inside a building after weaving our way through a bunch of corridors or underground?" Rivka asked.

"It doesn't change our engagement." Lindy made a finger gun and shot imaginary bad guys. "The most important thing for everyone to remember is that when we act, we need to take control of the situation. Once in control, we can leverage that to extricate ourselves if we are within layered security. I should say *when*, because there is no way the exchange will take place in the open."

"Which means we will take hostages," the dentist said slowly, closing his eyes and shaking his head.

"Criminals take hostages. We secure suspects. There is a monumental difference, because we assume responsibility for their health and well-being once in our custody."

"I'm good with that. Do I get a gun?" he asked. Red made a face, suggesting the answer was no.

"As with the best con jobs, it will be the appearance of being armed and not actually being armed. If there's a firefight, get between us and get down. You'll wear body armor under your clothes—the full set. It'll bulk you up to where they'll think you're a tough guy. Please understand that the last thing you want to do is shoot someone." Rivka gently put her hand on his shoulder. She didn't want the dentist to become like her or Red or Lindy.

"I get it. I'll try not to be in your way," he replied, sounding disappointed.

Hamlet appeared and wove his way between the legs of those standing. No one moved, since everyone had taken their turn getting tripped by the cat. Floyd bounced up and tried to touch noses, but Hamlet wasn't having any of that. He swiped a paw, but the wombat was nearly as quick, meeting his paw with her long-clawed foot. She grabbed his paw and tugged.

He yowled and jumped straight up. When he came back down, his back legs launched him toward the recliner where Rivka sat. She tried to dodge, but he was too quick, and she was trapped within the comfortable chair's confines. He ran up one leg, claws fully extended, before vaulting to his next victim.

When Hamlet ultimately landed in the corner of the room, he sat up and started grooming his face as if nothing had happened. There was much cursing, all of it directed at the white cat with gray spots.

Rivka waved to get everyone's attention.

"You are instrumental for us to maintain appearances," she told Tyler. "All of us are. Taking this ring down is the single most important effort we can make. Tomorrow, it may be something else, but for today, there are women who will never be kidnapped because Candi Matz is no more. If we eliminate the buyer on Fenek, more suppliers will be out of business. We eliminate enough suppliers, and the auction blocks on Corran will stand empty. Which reminds me, how much time until we have to be back for Seequa's hearing?"

"Five days, Magistrate," Chaz replied.

"Which means we have about two days to unfuck this planet. That's not a whole lot of time. I hope everyone got enough sleep."

"What is that supposed to mean?" Tyler whispered to Jay.

"It means, we may not get a chance to sleep again until we leave Fenek Eudoxius. Do you have your running shoes, Doc? She left off that part. We generally have to run."

"For fitness?"

"For our lives," Jay replied evenly.

Spinal Tap settled into its parking spot, one among a thousand other ships. The spaceport bustled with activity to feed visitors into and out of a dozen major cities that catered to a broad spectrum of activities from vacations to business and everything in between.

"How have I not heard of this place before?" Rivka asked while they waited to open the hatch and meet their ride.

"It is called Mecca colloquially. Fenek Eudoxius is the official name on star maps," Chaz replied.

"I've heard of Mecca. It's supposed to be where everyone wants to go," she intoned. It hadn't been on her wish list of places to visit.

"It's on our short list of places for a honeymoon," Lindy said.

"Probably won't be after we get done with it," Jay muttered under her breath.

"One of these days, people are going to like us after we've visited their planet," Rivka replied.

"But today is not that day!" Red declared.

Your transportation has arrived, Ankh noted using the internal comm chips relayed through *Spinal Tap's* system as a check to make sure they were functional.

The group delivered a variety of replies. All except the dentist, who lacked the chip.

"Doc says 'Roger,'" Rivka said for him. She hammered the hatch release with her fist and stepped in front of the outer door.

"Damn it, Magistrate!" Red shoved his way to the front as the first light appeared through the opening hatch. "Can't have you getting shot before you step foot on the planet."

"There would be a penalty to your paycheck," Rivka quipped, leaning back to allow Red to get in front.

He was first out the door and down the one step before hitting the pavement, stopping once there to scan for threats. "Stay close," he whispered over his shoulder. Rivka was right behind him, with Lindy close after. Jay, and finally Tyler left the ship. Chaz secured the hatch once the team was clear.

An aerial transport cab waited. Rectangular in shape, it was completely automated, with preset destinations based on the requestor's needs.

CRAIG MARTELLE & MICHAEL ANDERLE

Ankh, can you make sure this thing doesn't run us astray? Rivka requested.

Red led the way to the vehicle, head whipping back and forth as he maintained his vigilance.

Already on it, Ankh replied in his emotionless voice. *If it receives a changed destination, what are your instructions?*

Track it to its source while we go to the new location. Depending on where that is, we might need to retake control. I don't want to go off the grid. Even with this august group of warriors, the crime lords could dump us in an active volcano or somewhere equally unsavory. They had Candi and the one guard suicide when the slavers were nowhere near.

Noted, Ankh stated. Rivka knew he would keep them from being murdered as a group, but his ambiguous answers always ruffled her feathers. She wondered if he did it on purpose.

Probably not. Humans and the emotionally like-minded sentient races were probably as much a mystery to him as Crenellians were to them.

Thanks, Ankh, she allowed, knowing that he wouldn't reply.

The central area of the cab was for standing passengers, while seats followed a line around the inside of the walls. They entered the cab and filled the seats beneath the windows.

"We're pretty exposed," Red said to no one in particular.

"There's no way we won't be," Rivka remarked. The cab took off smoothly and accelerated toward the sky. Some traffic crawled along the ground, but most of the vehicles were airborne, giving the impression of stacks of traffic separated by a minimum amount of space.

"That's a lot of people," Jay said.

The dentist was all eyes as he took in the scenery.

"Don't get out much, Doc?" Rivka wondered aloud.

"Not to places like this," he answered, his childlike expression showing his fascination with the strange and wondrous city on the planet known as Mecca. Red and Lindy both frowned at the sheer volume of people.

Jay was trying to enjoy the ride, but as a slave to be sold, she shuddered at the thought of strangers appraising her like a piece of meat. The aircar bucked when it flew through a thermal and her stomach lurched. She covered her mouth to keep from throwing up.

Tyler hugged her to him.

Don't grow up to be like us, Rivka thought. *And as long as there are people like us, you won't have to.*

Rivka, rejoicing in the courage of her convictions, the foundation of her legal knowledge, and the abilities of those around her, set her jaw and watched the sprawling city go by. She wanted to answer the question of why she did this work. Besides Jhiordaan waiting for her had she turned down the High Chancellor, she was committed to Justice. Her gift wasn't hers, but to be used for the benefit of the galaxy.

The cab is on track to arrive at the original destination in three minutes, Ankh reported.

"Three minutes to touchdown. Mister Ch'ta'ka should be waiting for us somewhere down there."

Ankh had found the name in the only bits he could recover of a single deleted file within the nav computer of *Spinal Tap*. The Crenellian didn't believe in coincidences, so he'd had Erasmus make contact with Ch'ta'ka. The meeting had been arranged through a single message that received a one-word answer. "Done."

"I have no idea what to expect, so stay frosty, people. And keep her under guard. We can't have her running off before we close the deal." The Magistrate assumed the cab was bugged and that someone was listening in. They'd given nothing away so far, and would do what they had to in order to maintain appearances.

"She won't be going anywhere, *Candi*," Red replied, rolling his shoulders as he always did to get ready for expected action. He got up and bounced on the balls of his feet, and Lindy did the same as the adrenaline started to pump. Rivka stared out the window at the landing site they were approaching. Jay looked at the floor of the aircar, and the dentist watched her.

"Calmly," Rivka warned. Jay and Tyler both looked up and blinked away their hesitation. "Put on your game faces."

The cab touched down, and Red was first off. The others tumbled out behind him, staying in a tight circle. Rivka worked her way to the front, and they fell into the formation that Lindy had described earlier. Red and Lindy each kept one hand inside their jackets as they held onto their weapons. To the casual observer, it could have looked like a bluff.

To anyone who met their gaze, it would have been obvious that it was not. Rivka marched boldly toward the entrance that led from the pad.

The aerial cab lifted off.

No turning back now.

Check, check, Ankh are you there? Rivka asked.

I am, the Crenellian replied.

Do you have eyes on us?

I do not. There are no cameras observing this pad. The last image I have is from the cab.

We'll have to do this the hard way. We're going in. I'll stay in touch.

Rivka's smile was tight-lipped as she approached the door. A single dark-green alien appeared, holding out one of its four tentacle-like arms. It had an oversized head with two antennae, bug-eyes, and a tiny slit for a mouth. A metallic box hung around its neck.

"Hand her over," demanded a voice through the box. Rivka couldn't tell if the bug creature was talking or it was someone else and the bug was only transport for the communication device.

It motioned like a human, waving with one arm while pointing at Jay with another.

"We need to talk."

"No change. Hand her over," the voice from the box insisted.

"No change to what?"

"Same deal. Hand her over."

Rivka reached behind her and grabbed Jay by the arm. She winked at the young woman before she yanked her forward.

"Fine. Here you go." Rivka held Jay steady, keeping the girl slightly behind her as they approached the alien. The Magistrate let go of her arm and grabbed one of the tentacles. "Who do you work for?"

The alien recoiled quickly, but images popped into her mind. The box was a translator. The alien was the recovery thug. He would take her somewhere nearby for a handoff to other aliens.

Rivka jumped to get the best angle and powered a right cross into the bug's face. It collapsed onto itself, dazed by the blow. She hurried past it so the others could get out of the open. Red quickly secured the alien and tossed him aside, then started to walk away but stopped. He returned and removed the translator from around the alien's neck.

Rivka whispered to Jay, "Run down to the end, take a left, and follow it all the way to the bottom. There should be somebody down there. Take a look and then come back. I want to know what we're up against. The more we know, the fewer people will get hurt."

Jay looked at the corridor leading away from the door to the landing pad. She nodded and sprinted away, disappearing after the first couple of steps.

"Holy crap!" the dentist exclaimed. Jay reappeared before the last word was uttered.

"Three of them. One like the alien who met us and two four-legged Yollins."

"Yollins? And upper-class ones, at that. What kind of muscle did they have?"

"I didn't see anyone."

"How can you tell they're upper-class?" Tyler asked. Rivka ignored him as she concocted a plan.

Red tapped the dentist on the shoulder and held a finger to his lips. He whispered, "Lower-class only have two legs."

"The Yollins can't tell us what we need to know. Humans all look alike to them," Rivka explained.

"But they're expecting that guy," Tyler pointed to the bound alien.

"So right," she replied. "Won't be the first time we've had to bluff. Everyone ready?"

"What does that mean?" the dentist asked again, alarm overtaking his features.

Red held his finger to his lips again but didn't speak. He only shook his head. Tyler understood. He moved to the back of the group and stood immediately behind Jay, while Red and Lindy flanked her. Rivka strode boldly out front.

"Walk like we're supposed to be here. With a purpose, people," she encouraged. They stepped up to keep pace. She turned the corner and continued down the corridor. There were no exits. It led to only one place, and that had two Yollins and a third alien. She fixed them with her best stare and continued toward them.

The aliens were confused. They shuffled around briefly.

"Ho, there!" Rivka called. "Fuck that lackey you sent to meet me. I deliver in person!"

One of the Yollins stepped forward. "Stay where you are!" he ordered.

"Fuck you, too, buddy," she shot back, storming up to him despite his weapon being aimed at her. "Who do you work for?"

She grabbed his arm with one hand and tried to rip the weapon from his other, but he wouldn't let go. They struggled while she listened in on his thoughts. Shocked, she stepped back.

"Fuck you, human!" The Yollin backed away. The three of them continued to walk backward until they disappeared into an elevator.

CRAIG MARTELLE & MICHAEL ANDERLE

"Why did you let them go?" Red asked.

"I...I have what I need. We have to get back to the ship *now!*"

Ankh, call us a cab and prepare for immediate departure. Forget the cab. Have Chaz fly the shuttle over here and pick us up right fucking now!

May I ask why? Ankh queried before adding, *Stairs are retracted. We have lift-off.* Spinal Tap *will be there in two minutes at maximum acceleration.*

We'll discuss it after we leave orbit.

"What's going on?" Tyler asked as the group jogged up the corridor on their way to the exit. The alien was still bound, but he was awake. They didn't give him a second look as they passed, leaving him where he was.

The shuttle appeared as a dot in the distance that was screaming past the other air traffic. It avoided getting in an accident, performing a high-gee maneuver to stop in a hover above the pad, then it dropped to the pad and the hatch opened. The team hurried aboard. Chaz was already airborne again before the hatch secured. He pointed the nose upward, racing for orbit and beyond.

"Straight to *Peacekeeper*, Chaz," the Magistrate ordered.

Red and Lindy gave Rivka her space. Jay and Tyler wanted to know why the operation was canceled so abruptly.

Rivka's lips turned white from clamping them shut. She tried to relax, but she was having trouble. She closed her eyes and tried to force herself to be calm. "In his mind, I saw some of the people he was working for. One of them was the High Chancellor."

CHAPTER TWELVE

No one spoke until after they rendezvoused with *Peacekeeper*. Even then, Rivka kept her own counsel. As soon as they boarded, they ditched the long-range shuttle at the edge of Fenek's space. Rivka stormed the bridge, carried Ankh out, and secured the door behind her.

The Crenellian looked as stoic as usual. He turned to Red, craning his neck to look up at the big man.

"She needs to have a private conversation with Grainger, I suspect," Red offered. "I think the High Chancellor is involved somehow."

Ankh studied Red as if questioning the veracity of his claim. Once he realized that he was sincere, Ankh replied, "I don't."

He moved to the kitchen, where the blank look on his face suggested he was talking to Erasmus. The food processor dinged, and a hot meal appeared.

"Why can't you hook us up with some of that?" Red pleaded.

"By 'us,' you mean you. There's only a limited amount of

source matter for these types of meals. You would consume it all in a matter of hours. If only I eat them, it will last weeks."

"You're a little dude," Red blurted. Lindy slapped her forehead.

"That's not the point."

"What I hear is that we need more of that source matter. Tell me what it is and I'll get it, come hell or high water. Then will you share?"

"Probably not."

"You little cretin!"

"So big, and you haul around such a tiny brain. What a shame." Ankh stood with his tiny legs shoulder-width apart and stared the big man down.

Lindy smiled at the Crenellian. He didn't respond.

Red started to reach for him, but Lindy caught his arm. Red looked ashamed.

"I'm sorry, Ankh. You are a bigger man than me." Red returned to the rec room and set up the weight bench, in search of a way to burn off the energy that coursed through his veins. He didn't know what would come of the Magistrate's conversation. He didn't even know with whom she'd be talking. His job was to be ready when she took action.

He started pounding out reps.

"Let me know what you need to source the food processor, and we'll obtain as much of it as the system can hold," Lindy said softly, taking a knee so she could look the Crenellian in the eye.

Jay appeared with the dentist. "If you give us a list of meals, we can build a supply to have a set menu. I don't think 'catch as catch can' and 'grab what you want' are keeping us close as a crew. We should have set meals, and that way, we can help Floyd to keep from overeating. She's gotten a little plump since she's joined the crew."

No! More pizza, Floyd called.

"I think what you meant to say was no more pizza, and you'd be right. A lean Floyd is a happy Floyd."

Snorting and grunting, the wombat shuffled away.

"A gorged Floyd is a happy Floyd, just like a gorged Red," the big man remarked. "It takes a lot of fuel to run this engine."

Everyone looked at him. No one said anything.

Finally, the dentist asked what they were all thinking but trying to avoid. "Do we have to go after the High Chancellor now?"

"Why do you always call in the middle of the night?"

"Because that's when the shit that's out of my control happens," Rivka replied.

"Tell me again what you think you saw?"

"That's pretty demeaning. I'll tell you what I saw. How we interpret it could have a significant impact on the galaxy. Do we bring General Reynolds or Nathan Lowell in on it?"

"In on what?" Grainger asked.

"The High Chancellor figuring prominently in the mind of a slave trader!" Rivka exclaimed.

"Describe it again," Grainger said patiently as he tried to rub the sleep from his eyes.

"I asked a four-legged Yollin who he worked for. In his mind were images of other Yollins and Corranites, and an image of the High Chancellor appeared before he pulled away. I only asked the one question. The way it works is, the questions bring their thoughts to the surface. The stronger the surprise, the less guarded they are. If they are ready for it, their thoughts are about how they want to murder me or the like. It can be disturbing. If anyone ever offers you the power to see into someone else's mind, turn them down."

"I understand, Zombie. I wouldn't want that. Back to what you saw. Did this Yollin meet with the High Chancellor?"

"The memories were his, seen through his own eyes."

"Do you have pictures of the Yollin?" Grainger asked.

"No. We were undercover and traveling lean. We didn't know what kind of counter-surveillance technology they had, so we didn't risk it."

"You have no evidence?"

"I have all the evidence a Magistrate needs, which is what I personally saw."

"Which is nothing. Are you willing to drop it?"

"Are you smoking *xinqal* weed?"

"Not smoking anything. What do you want to do?"

"And that's why I called—because I have no idea. Why was High Chancellor Wyatt talking with traffickers?"

"They are Yollins. His office is on Yoll. It could have been any function the High Chancellor attended."

"We need to ask him," Rivka declared. "But discreetly..."

Grainger grunted his understanding of the situation. "By 'we,' you mean me. And by 'discreetly,' you mean that I need to go to Yoll and talk to the High Chancellor in person. Send me your report on this case, as much as you have."

Rivka nodded her agreement. "I owe you one. You can't imagine how much grief this is causing me."

"Because we like to believe that those in charge of us are as upright as we are?"

"A system with corrupt people is corrupted, no matter what they say. It would call into question everything we've done. We would go down with our higher-ups. The Federation can't withstand something like that. The scumbag power brokers would fill the leadership void. How many would die from such a societal collapse? We need a solid framework within which everyone can work. It's like a contract where one party doesn't trust the other and there are no enforceability provisions."

"It wouldn't be worth the digital space it occupied."

"Looks like I'm going to the royal city of Khn'Chik on Yoll," Grainger grumbled briefly before continuing. "Gotta go, Zombie. Send me that report. Expect the best, prepare for the worst."

"What do you mean by that?" Rivka asked, leaning forward to glare at the screen.

"Take down the traffickers. Kill the slave trade, and let's see if the General can bring Corran into the Federation." The screen went blank. Rivka hung her head, the weight of her fears taking its toll. She forced herself to stand, collecting her thoughts before going back to the rec room to face the others.

When she opened the hatch and looked toward the rec room, her team was waiting without pushing her. Their patience warmed her heart. She stepped over the hatch's knee-knocker, the lower structure that helped seal the bridge off from the rest of the ship, and joined her team.

"We are staying on the case and following the leads while Grainger goes to Yoll to talk to the High Chancellor."

Red loosened his collar because of a sudden increase in heat.

Or the perception that it was getting hotter. Jay started to cry, and Tyler was there instantly, draping an arm around her shoulders and helping her to sit down. Floyd raced in and almost knocked her down as she flew into Jay's chest to nuzzle and comfort her.

Lindy clenched her jaw and spoke through gritted teeth. "If he's involved in the slave trade, fuck him. If he has any role, I'll be happy to drag him from his seat of power and throw him on the floor. But as you've taught us, Magistrate, we have to assume that he's innocent. Did you see him take money from slavers or hand over a slave?"

"I did not," Rivka confirmed.

"Then we protect him. Either he's guilty or not. There is no in-between. We take him down or wish him well on his way."

Red looked like a proud father. "What she said," he added.

Rivka chuckled.

"I remember a time not long ago where you said that you would protect me and all the legal stuff was my responsibility."

"Times change, but I think you are misremembering. You spoke those words. It was the 'stay in your landing pattern' speech," Red replied. "But we don't have the luxury of staying in one exhaust manifold. We all have to do each other's jobs if that's what it takes to complete the mission."

Rivka gave him the side-eye.

"Mission," Red enunciated slowly.

Ankh took a step forward so everyone could hear him. "You get me the names and faces of those Yollin, and I will find where their paths have crossed the High Chancellor's."

Rivka tried to recall their faces to transmit an image to the Crenellian, but too much time had passed. Their faces were no longer clear enough in her mind. "Chaz, take *Peacekeeper* back to Fenek, best possible speed. Set up a meeting with local law enforcement as soon as we arrive."

"I feel much more comfortable this way," Red said to Lindy. She nodded in agreement as they checked each other over one last time before touchdown. They wore their full ballistic protection and carried railguns, and they were armed with grenades in addition to the maximum load of explosives and ammunition. The bodyguards were geared for war.

Just in case the Yollins wanted to put up a fight.

Rivka looked at Tyler and Jay. "Are you sure?"

Tyler shook his head. "If I were to wait until I was certain, I'd still be back there." He pointed with his thumb over his shoulder at the rec room. "We're a team, right?"

"Don't get killed," she warned him.

He laughed the nervous laugh of someone forced to listen to a tasteless joke. Jay slapped him on the shoulder. "I'll watch your back, Doc."

"What's up with that disappearing?" he asked out of the blue, suddenly interested after forgetting about it with their rapid departure on their previous trip.

"I can run really fast. You lose sight of me. But I'm not strong like them." Jay nodded at the Magistrate and her bodyguards. "It's the nanocytes. Ankh made me special. He wanted to give me something that would work best with my personality. I can't imagine what I'd use extra strength for, but Ankh—he knows that I would prefer to run away from trouble than fight my way out."

"Fire in the hole!" Red called as he mashed the big red button. The hatch opened, and stairs extended. He walked into the daylight, head on a swivel as he took in their surroundings. He breathed deeply, as he always did once outside—a last check of the air before the Magistrate took in a lungful.

As before, an aerial cab waited at the edge of the parking apron.

Lindy followed Red and Rivka was close behind, happy to once again be wearing her Magistrate's jacket. The bistok leather felt good against her skin. She vowed not to waste time going undercover again. Her position was a final arbiter of Justice in a galaxy where perps could disappear at a moment's notice. And disappear forever.

She needed to wear the authority of her station. If Justice needed to be administered, she could do it right there. Even given the wisdom of allowing the small crimes that would lead to a kingpin, she still couldn't do it.

She would follow the leads generated through her gift, counting on the velocity of their engagements to follow the trail to those worth taking down. She would not just gut the organization, she would put away everyone associated with it.

That was why she needed the local law enforcement. They would collect the bodies left in her wake.

I hope you get to the bottom of it, Grainger, she prayed. The last thing the Magistrate wanted was to think of the man she looked up to as corrupt. It had already shaken her confidence in the system.

Who watches the watchers?

Why do we do what we do?

The questions seemed to be linked.

If they have to watch us, should we be doing what we do? If I didn't have to answer to the High Chancellor, would I be attentive to the rules?

Rivka missed the majority of the cab's flight, snapping back into the moment when they landed.

"Standard departure and approach," Red ordered. When it came to the Magistrate's security, he was in charge. "It's showtime."

He stepped out and made a beeline for the entrance to the law enforcement station. As with most buildings on this part of Fenek Eudoxius, the cab had delivered them to one of a seemingly infinite number of landing pads attached to a massive complex centered on a main skyscraper.

The others spread around, the dentist bringing up the rear since he wasn't used to wearing a complete set of body armor and he was more out of shape than he wanted to admit. Jay smiled and motioned for him to catch up. He breathed heavily, willing himself to keep pace.

Jay winked at him and turned her attention back to the

door through which they'd enter. Red was already there and holding it for Lindy to make sure it was safe for the Magistrate to enter. Sounds of a struggle filtered through. Red held out his hand to stop Rivka and ran inside, letting the door close behind him. She turned to see if they could get back to the cab.

The vehicle had already flown away.

CHAPTER THIRTEEN

The Royal City of Khn'Chik on Yoll

Grainger wasn't used to waiting in a long line of spaceships to enter the landing pattern. The megacity below was one of many on the system's central planet. The Yollins had once led a vast empire.

That was until they met Bethany Anne, the human who would defeat the emperor and unseat the upper class. The system she put in its place grew stronger with each passing day because of the loyalists, those who put honor and Justice before anything else. It was said that the leader only sets the stage. Those who surround them determine what is.

Or what is not.

The thought of corruption at the highest levels of the Etheric Federation's leadership was unfathomable. Grainger had been on the inside before the Rangers were disbanded. He'd seen what it was like, and he'd agreed with their charter back then. He agreed with the Magistrates' charter now.

Like the Knights of the Round Table in their service to king and country, Grainger lived to serve, but he dedicated his life's work to the Queen. As had the High Chancellor.

"We are fourth in the pattern," Beau announced. The Frigate's artificial intelligence flew the ship in addition to handling the myriad research and planning tasks Grainger required. Theirs was a mutually beneficial arrangement since Beau liked to travel.

Had he not liked it, there could have been serious issues because he was integrated with the frigate—a ship without a name, only a number. Lucky number 69 as Grainger would say to snickers and chortles.

"Do we have what we need to get to the High Chancellor's office?" Grainger asked.

"Of course. Your vehicle will be waiting for you the second you disembark. There is room on the High Chancellor's schedule fifteen minutes after that. Our delay has cut into your transit time, but you should make it."

"I *should* make it," Grainger emphasized. "But I don't want to show up completely unannounced. I just want to get this over with. Beau, connect me to the High Chancellor's assistant."

A raspy voice answered almost immediately. "High Chancellor Wyatt's office, this is Zai'den. How can I help you?"

"Magistrate Grainger, and I'd like to meet with the High Chancellor as soon as possible."

"He is available now. May I share with him your topic?"

"We're in the landing pattern. I believe I can be there in about twenty minutes." Beau flashed green lights to let

Grainger know that his estimate was sound. "The topic is a private matter that I can't discuss over an open channel."

"Very well, Master Grainger."

"Magistrate..." The line went dead before he could correct the Yollin assistant. Grainger didn't know why he was uncomfortable dealing with a Yollin assistant to the High Chancellor. They were on Yoll, after all.

69 touched down, and the door opened to a sunny day. Khn'Chik presented an impressive array of soaring spires and great buildings constructed in such a way as to appear carved from stone. The warmth of the day welcomed him, but he wished it were cooler. The heat bore down on his soul, encouraging the fire he fought to hold back.

He walked with purpose to the waiting vehicle and climbed in. It took off the moment he was belted in. A quick twelve minutes later, it had parked and discharged its lone passenger. Grainger headed for the main door of the Etheric Federation administrative center, a building capable of housing a thousand personnel performing the necessary functions of running a group that claimed responsibility for a trillion lives.

The number was nearly incomprehensible. The Magistrates had the inauspicious task of prosecuting criminals who wreaked havoc on the Federation's ideals, like those who killed ambassadors. Or those who ran the slave trade.

Once inside, an interactive screen gave Grainger directions to the High Chancellor's office. He passed through a number of security checkpoints on his way, but when he arrived, he felt like it hadn't been a burden or harassment. The Yollin guards were professional and polite.

The executive assistant was the same, asking Grainger if he wanted a cup of tea or a Coke before seeing the High Chancellor. The Magistrate shook his head, the blood pounding in his ears as he prepared to engage his leader on an issue where the only evidence suggested he was corrupt.

Zai'den opened the door, holding it for Grainger to walk woodenly through and closing it behind him with the finality of a funeral dirge.

High Chancellor Wyatt smiled pleasantly upon the Magistrate's arrival. He stood and walked around his desk, hand offered in greeting.

Grainger shook it but didn't speak.

Wyatt assessed the expression on the Magistrate's face. "What brings you here?" he asked bluntly.

Grainger thought of ways to obfuscate, of small talk that would take time so he could think of something, but none of it made any sense. He needed it to be over. "Rivka found evidence of you in the company of Yollin slavers..." Grainger didn't continue. He made no accusation and asked no question. He simply put a fact on the table where they could both look at it.

The Magistrate smelled sandalwood and the must of old books, even though he could see none as he looked around, wondering about the scent and why it would attract his attention. He met the High Chancellor's gaze. The older man was waiting for him to turn back so he could look Grainger in the eye.

"I wondered when she would find out about that," he started.

. . .

Mecca, Planet Fenek Eudoxius

Rivka rushed to the closed door and crouched behind it. Jay and Tyler hovered nearby, shielding her from view.

"Oh, fuck no!" she declared, looking at who she was hiding behind. "Follow me." She grabbed the door and yanked it open, jumping inside to find a standoff. Three uniformed officers were down, while six more had weapons trained on Lindy and Red, who were standing back to back, aiming their railguns.

"All right, everyone calm down!" she stated loudly, holding her hands in up what she hoped was the universal gesture for peace.

"Has anyone ever calmed down because you told them to?" Red mumbled.

Rivka ignored him. "I'm going to reach into my pocket and pull out my credentials. I'm Magistrate Rivka Anoa, protected under Federation Laws, Appendix D, Chapter Seven, Section 1. I have diplomatic protection, and as such, I rate armed guards at all times. I'm glad no one was shot since I would hate to have to explain why all of you got yourselves killed."

"Is this how she defuses a situation?" Tyler whispered to Jay.

"Pretty much," the young woman replied out the side of her mouth. They both held their hands in the air, having conceded that they didn't want to get shot.

Rivka slowly removed her credentials let them drop open and walked toward the officer wearing the most slashes and badges, assuming him to be the ranking member of the welcoming committee.

"Put your railguns down, please," Rivka encouraged Red & Lindy. They exhaled together and stood up straight, letting the business ends of their weapons drop to point at the floor.

The officers relaxed but maintained their aim.

"You can see the credentials, so it's okay if you order your people to stand down. Otherwise, I'm going to have a serious conversation with your superiors. And I will start at the top. I believe you have a president on this planet. I'll go to his office, and we'll talk. Or, you could get your shit under control right now, and we'll call this little misunderstanding concluded."

The older Fenek holstered his weapon, and the others followed suit. None of them looked happy, but Rivka couldn't tell from their humanoid faces. They gave nothing away. She found the small tentacles they sported in lieu of facial hair to be disconcerting.

"You could have sent a message that you were coming and we would have been expecting you," the senior officer told her.

"We did, but only about twenty minutes ago. We need to see your senior commissioner since we are on urgent business."

"You can't see him armed like that."

"This again," Rivka muttered looking over her shoulder at Red. He shook his head. She turned back to the Fenek. "Do you understand the authority of a Magistrate?"

"I believe I do," he replied.

"Then point us in the direction of the commissioner, if you would be so kind. We're all going. Don't make me lodge a formal complaint."

"They can't go." He put his foot down, crossed his arms, and stood in the center of the hallway.

Rivka removed her datapad. "Your name?"

"Klavin," he belted out boldly.

"Klavin," she said slowly as she typed it in, then activated the comm link. "Chaz, if you would be so kind, please transmit my disappointment to the president regarding my reception at Law Enforcement Central. Also, attach the name and face you see here as an individual who ordered weapons pointed at me and my security and is currently in violation of Appendix D, Chapter 7, Section 1. Federation agents will be taking him into custody shortly."

His expression showed mild amusement.

The datapad vibrated a few moments later. Rivka looked at the screen. "Mister President," she greeted with a smile.

"Please accept my personal apologies, Magistrate Anoa. You'll be extended every courtesy due your station, and if there is anything I can do to assist in your current case, please don't hesitate to ask."

"Thank you, Mister President. As a matter of fact, I have had no luck convincing Officer Klavin to let me through for my appointment with the commissioner. Maybe you could talk to him."

Rivka spun the datapad around and shoved it toward the officer's face.

"Mister President," he stammered.

"Klavin. You're embarrassing me and all of Fenek Eudoxius. You will escort the Magistrate everywhere she needs to go to make sure they understand that she's acting

CRAIG MARTELLE & MICHAEL ANDERLE

under my personal authority. Do you understand, or do I have to promote someone else in your place?"

"No, sir!" the officer nearly shouted.

"Good!" the president declared. Rivka cocked one eyebrow as Klavin, now shaken, handed the datapad over.

"Please, follow me," he said, bowing respectfully before angrily motioning for the other officers to go away.

You're a genius, Ankh, Rivka relayed using their internal comm. *Did you even contact the president?*

No, the Crenellian replied.

I expect we'll be finished before anyone suspects anything. We have less than two days to wrap things up.

My thoughts exactly. Please hurry, Magistrate, Ankh told her.

Rivka looked troubled as she followed the officer through the corridors to the commissioner's chamber, a grand and luxurious suite with a small buffet of snacks in the outer office.

Red eyed the food with limited curiosity. He was still unsure if the locals were friendly or hostile, so he kept his finger alongside the trigger guard on his railgun, his muscles relaxed but ready. He met Lindy's gaze; she was as taut as a piano wire. Something didn't smell right, but they didn't know what it was.

The Magistrate followed Klavin past the snacks and into the office, motioning for the others to remain behind. Red gritted his teeth and chose to stand next to the door. The officer and the big bodyguard glared at each other until Klavin closed the door in Red's face. Jay and Tyler sat down on an overstuffed couch and looked bored. Lindy grabbed a snack and stuffed it quickly into her mouth.

She gagged and covered her mouth, depositing the ill-advised treat in the trash.

Red looked at her questioningly.

"They weren't chocolate chips."

Finally, Red lightened up as he continued to lean against the door, trying to hear what was happening beyond, but it was too stout. He could hear nothing.

"Welcome, Magistrate Anoa. I wish we would have known you were coming to avoid any unpleasantness. We apologize profusely for any discomfort we caused you."

"We notified you. I have no idea what your people did with the notification once it was transmitted. I would have thought Mecca would be more efficient." She let that rest with him, but he didn't squirm. He sat stoically, as if it were business as usual.

"I didn't see your request, so you'll have to tell me what you are here for. I appreciate your patience and understanding," he replied smoothly.

She was happy that he didn't blame any of his people, especially since she hadn't sent a request.

So much bluffing on this case, but if slave traders have their tentacles in the highest levels of the government, no one is above suspicion.

No one.

"We have evidence suggesting that traffickers are using Fenek Eudoxius as a hub through which to bring in sentient capital and then export those victims to Corran.

There are a couple Yollins that I am particularly interested in finding."

"We have a large population of Yollins, so much so that they have their own security element. If you give us the names of those under investigation, we'll forward that information to the appropriate group."

"I don't have their names or pictures. I only have their faces in my mind. They were last seen in the Balurian sector of the city."

"That's not much to go on. What are you *really* after, Magistrate?" The commissioner leaned forward, elbows on his desk and fingers steepled before him.

"I want the kingpin, and I believe he or she is here."

"That's a bold claim, Magistrate, and it doesn't sound like you have the evidence to support it. A hunch?"

"A good hunch. We've intercepted people coming here as well as leaving here. They suicided rather than talk to us. Forensic analysis of their ships provided us with almost no data."

"Almost. What did you find?" he asked, appearing to take an interest.

"An entity named Ch'ta'ka," Rivka revealed.

The commissioner accessed his system to input the name. A few moments later, he returned his attention to Rivka. "It appears this Ch'ta'ka is a person of interest to us as well."

"I would love to talk to him."

"It is in hiding, but rest assured, should it show its face, we'll be there." The commissioner didn't sound convincing.

"I have the best digital analysts in the 'verse on my ship. Please send me any details you have on this individual, and my guy will be able to find it. What race is it, by the way?"

"Ch'ta'ka is an Auroran, one of the exoskeleton-type species. Similar to a Yollin, but without the mandibles."

The commissioner focused his attention on his screen. Rivka leaned forward as if trying to see, reaching under the desk to hold Ankh's disc as close to the computer as possible. The screen flashed and returned to normal. The commissioner paused with his hands in the air.

Rivka froze, slowly palming the disc to secret it away.

"I swear, so much for newfangled electronics. If I touch it, it breaks. Maybe it's a gift." He chuckled and poked a few more commands into his computer.

"Let me look at my pad and see if the information has gone through." The Magistrate dropped the disc into the inside pocket as she retrieved her datapad and tapped a quick note to Ankh.

I have it all, he replied.

"He's on it now, Commissioner. I can't thank you enough. I believe Klavin has been assigned to escort me?"

"So I hear," the commissioner conceded. "Whatever you need, let him know, and he'll take care of it. How many days are you going to be here?"

"I think hours is the right answer. I have an appointment on Corran that I cannot be late for. A human's life hangs in the balance," she noted, giving him extra information to earn his trust.

"Just one human?"

"She is the way through the barrier blocking us from a non-Federation planet. Through her, we can remove a major supplier of potential victims. All sentient species who have been sold into slavery will benefit from this one Federation citizen. The dominos will fall quickly when the correct first one is toppled." Rivka leaned back in her seat.

Her datapad buzzed, notifying her that Ankh had two potential locations. "Shall we go talk to Ch'ta'ka?" she asked.

The commissioner was confused. He canted his head and gave her a blank look.

"We have two potential locations, both of which border the Yollin district within the Balurian sector. Data suggests both sites are active right now. The quicker we move, the quicker we'll be able to get our answers and get out of your hair—I mean tentacles."

"We call them 'hair,' for your reference." The commissioner smiled. "Give me the addresses. Klavin, go with the Magistrate to the other. Take a couple of officers with you, and I'll send an ORT to the second location."

"ORT?" Rivka wondered, showing Klavin on her datapad which address had the higher probability of containing the Auroran and his Yollin lackeys.

"Outlaw Recovery Team," Klavin said before giving the second address to the commissioner.

He tapped his interface and spoke softly toward his input device. "You better hurry. The ORT will deploy in less than two minutes. They are highly disciplined and well-trained." The commissioner waved as Rivka jumped from her seat and headed for the door, opening it for Klavin to rush out.

"The game is afoot!" Rivka cried triumphantly before she ran after the officer. The others were up in an instant and sprinting behind her.

"I guess you have a lead?" the dentist asked, taking a breath after every two words. "You weren't kidding. We *are* running!"

Jay laughed and hooked an arm under the dentist's to help him pick up the pace.

"We might get the Yollins and Ch'ta'ka all at one time," Rivka called over her shoulder.

CHAPTER FOURTEEN

The Royal City of Khn'Chik on Yoll

Grainger nervously chewed the inside of his lip. He was in no hurry to push the High Chancellor. The older man sat down in his chair, dignity intact, shoulders back and head held high.

"There was a time not long ago that I fancied myself the equal of Magistrates." He stopped to fix Grainger with his piercing eyes. To Grainger's credit, he didn't flinch or succumb to the pressure. He simply waited. Behind his calm exterior, his mind raced. He came to the conclusion that there was nothing he could do besides ask questions to understand.

"The slave trade didn't start here, but Yoll sure as hell didn't discourage it. But I believed that there was a hierarchy. I thought I would work my way to the top and take it down. You know how you do that?"

Grainger wasn't comfortable speaking since he didn't know where the High Chancellor was going, so he simply shook his head.

"You start at the bottom and get cozy with the lackeys, but I'm High Chancellor Wyatt! I don't start at the bottom." The older man hammered his fist into his hand and gritted his teeth. "They played me for the fool I was. I backed out, but not before they'd already gotten plenty of pictures. They laughed at me—and I deserved it."

"I can't believe you let them blackmail you," Grainger blurted before he could catch himself. He took a deep breath and forced himself to sit back. Somewhere outside the window, a siren blared.

"They never played that card. I sensed it was coming, which was why Rivka got handed this case. Only through serendipity did she find that human woman on Corran. That opened the gates through which we can pour resources."

"I didn't see any additional resources allocated to this case." Grainger groaned and stared at the wall.

"Don't feel bad, Magistrate Grainger. Verify what I'm telling you. General Reynolds has increased his engagement to get Corran to join the Federation. He's going to kill the slave trade from that side, while Rivka kills it on our side."

"Then you'll be free, and no one will know what you did?" Grainger didn't want to accuse the High Chancellor, but he did it anyway.

Wyatt didn't answer. He mirrored Grainger's expression, an interrogation technique to put the opposite party at ease.

"Did any of your actions result in the illegal detention and transport of an unwilling party?"

"Did I break the law?" the High Chancellor clarified. "Not as far as I know."

Grainger relaxed, sighing in relief.

"What do they have on you? Are you compromised?"

High Chancellor Wyatt stood, straightened his jacket, and strolled to the window with his hands clasped behind his back. He looked out for a long while. Grainger considered joining him so they could look outside while talking instead of at each other.

Grainger was used to questioning suspects, but he couldn't look at the High Chancellor as a suspect or a victim.

"I am an old man who has done this job for too many years to count. But I still love it. I love the effect that good laws have on a society. A better understanding of the boundaries means fewer people inadvertently violate them. We only want to invest our time dealing with real criminals. Those who refuse to be constrained by societal norms. Those we would call psychopaths. They are the ones we need to address. The traffickers? The ones we see are the mules—the hired muscle. We want the ones paying their salaries. Those are the ones we don't see, and we have to go in after them and dig them out."

Wyatt turned, his expression grimly determined.

"Those are the ones we must judge and sanction. They cannot be allowed to breathe the same air as free men."

Grainger nodded slowly. "What's next, High Chancellor?"

"I'm going back in as their lackey, but this time you'll be watching, and with our trusty security force, rolling up everyone in the organization. We'll flush the bastards into the open because we'll eliminate their workers. They'll have to come into the light to recruit new hands. If we chase them off Yoll, all the better."

"What's going to make this time different?" Grainger wondered.

"This time there won't be hesitation or pandering. This time I'm going to clean house." The High Chancellor cracked his knuckles.

"*We*," Grainger corrected.

Balurian Sector, Mecca, Planet Fenek Eudoxius

Peacekeeper raced in, flaring in a stomach-lurching maneuver before touching down with the door open and stairs extending in a single motion. Klavin ran off first, with Rivka and her team following closely behind.

All the buildings were massive structures. Residences were apartments within them. Some had gardens and greenery integrated into the buildings, making it appear as if they were more than a building. Artistic illusion; a designer's sleight of hand.

It was a concrete jungle, a massive city designed to be convenient for those who lived within it. Gardens and parks gave the appearance of being one with nature, and the residents were happy. It gave them what they needed. Work. Fulfillment. Entertainment. Friends a short ride away. The like-minded congregated in certain areas, and those sections of the city became known for the alien majorities who lived there.

Like where they were headed. Klavin referred to it as Yollin Town. Specialty shops catered to those from Yoll.

Housing was made to look like that in the megacities of the home planet.

Aliens gravitated toward their own to ease the transition from their homeworlds to a new planet. After being in Mecca for a while, many moved into higher-class areas, integrating with the general population. No one cared if a Yollin lived next to a Fenek, who lived next to a human.

Everyone lived for the opportunity to better the lives of their families.

Until someone like Ch'ta'ka tore someone away and sold them into slavery. The unwitting believed that their service would relieve the burden on their family. They didn't know that the burden was created by those who would exploit them.

"This individual has a lot to answer for," Rivka mumbled. Klavin entered the main door and took a hard turn into one of four corridors. He acted like he knew where he was going.

Red was immediately on high alert, scanning the walls for any kind of sign that would indicate where the target residence was located. He found nothing. Two more sharp turns later, Klavin pointed. Rivka closed with him and grabbed his arm.

"How did you know where this place was?" she demanded.

"All buildings have the same numbering design, right to left, small to large, fractions of the total units within a building. First number is the floor," he explained with a shrug, looking pointedly at her hand.

She sensed no deception. "I'm sorry. This whole thing has me on edge." She let go and held her hands up. She nodded to Red and Lindy to let them know it was okay. They visibly relaxed but maintained vigil with their railguns pointed at the walls.

Officer Klavin saw Rivka look at the bodyguards. "You probably shouldn't fire those in here. No matter which way you fire, there will always be someone behind them. This is a rather large city, and we are surrounded by millions of beings," he explained, not sounding demeaning. He didn't want any collateral damage. No one wanted to hurt an innocent.

Red and Lindy slung their railguns and hoisted their hand blasters. The entire process took no more than two seconds.

Rivka appreciated the professionals on her team. Jay and the dentist stood farther back, choosing to stay out of the way but being there in case they needed Jay's speed or Tyler's medical skill. The Magistrate carried Reaper in her hand. She wasn't going to let anyone get away. Better for her to lose the ability to interrogate them than let a trafficker run free.

The lawyer in her was appalled. She had no evidence that Ch'ta'ka was a slaver. She knew the two Yollins were players in the game. She needed to know where they stood, and wanted to talk to anyone in their company.

Ankh had given this address a higher than ninety percent probability that they would find Ch'ta'ka. She hadn't shared that tidbit with the commissioner, but it didn't matter. They would bracket the suspects and bring them in.

Then she would do her thing.

Klavin stood outside the door with an officer's master

pass in his hand. With it, he could open any door in the city. When the team nodded that they were ready, he waved it in front of the keypad.

Nothing happened. He tapped it and pushed. The door remained closed. "That's illegal!" he stated as he looked dumbly at the pad.

Red fired one round into the locking mechanism and followed by lunging forward and driving his foot into the door. It squealed and twisted, but it didn't burst open. It took a second kick to widen the gap enough for Klavin to squeeze through, with Rivka close behind him. Lindy squirmed after them, almost getting stuck. Red attacked the door with his shoulder, but it would open no farther.

"Halt!" Klavin bellowed at the Aurorans within. "In the name of Meccan Law Enforcement, you will freeze!"

That only energized those inside to step up their efforts to be in any other room than where they were. Rivka sprinted across the open space toward the one who looked to be in charge. Someone fired a weapon, and two quick rounds cracked past Rivka's head and slammed into the chest carapace of an Auroran with a hand blaster. One round thudded hard against a heavy ridge in the shell, while the other found a softer spot. Black ichor spilled from the hole as the shooter fell. More shots thundered within the confines of the apartment.

Klavin never drew his weapon. He dodged and seized two who were trying to squeeze through a door at the same time. He smashed their heads together, demonstrating an uncanny, nearly nanocyte-driven power.

Rivka dragged her target to the deck. He struggled for

only a moment, but he had landed on his face and the Magistrate had his arms pinned. "Where's Ch'ta'ka?"

She was rewarded by the image of the Auroran on the floor.

"Got him," she announced, ducking to stay out of the line of fire, but one, two, and then a third round slammed into her body armor. With an adrenaline-fueled fury, she lifted Ch'ta'ka and threw him to the side, following him to pin him in a corner, away from the lines of fire.

Klavin was against the opposite wall, holding his side where the light red blood of his species covered his hand and dripped to the floor. Lindy was crouched behind a chair and fired regularly to throw off their attackers' aim.

With a primal scream, Red burst through the door, rolled his railgun off his shoulder, and standing in the open, snapped three shots at the figures trying to hide. The hypervelocity darts exploded through the Aurorans' natural armor, spraying clouds of black lifeblood on the far wall. The darts embedded, not having enough remaining energy to penetrate. Red slung his weapon while he bolted forward. Pointing at the right door, he plunged through the one on the left.

Lindy followed him and his signal, cutting through the doorway on the right.

"Clear!" Red called.

"Runners! And they're Yollins," Lindy yelled back as her footsteps pounded away.

"Mine," Jay said, and disappeared. Tyler hurried to Klavin's side and urged him to sit.

"I don't know your anatomy. Do you have any organs in this area?" the dentist asked.

"Only important ones," he gasped, his breathing growing more ragged with each passing heartbeat.

"How do I call for emergency help?"

"I'm linked to the station. They should already know I'm in distress," he answered, despite the pain it caused him to speak. The doc put pressure on the wound, but the bleeding didn't slow. "Cauterize."

Klavin lost consciousness with the last word.

"I need heat!" Tyler demanded. Red tossed him a micro-welder before returning to his examination of the dead bodies, remaining close to the Magistrate. Her security was his paramount concern. His eyes kept shifting toward the doorway leading to the back exit. He could hear Lindy growling at someone, followed by the hollow-melon sound of a fist punching someone in the side of the head.

Tyler pulled his pocket knife and used the blue tip of the flame to superheat the blade, then touched it across the wound, burning the flesh together while turning the blood into black coagulated ash. He heated the blade again, burning off the blood and skin before applying it to the wound a second time.

He wiped the blade on his own pants when it was cool enough, then sat back and hoped the emergency medical team would arrive quickly.

"Get in there!" Lindy snarled. A body hit the floor, and a Yollin's head slid through the opening. Red grabbed the suspect by his mandible and dragged him into the main room. He drove a knee into the middle of the Yollin's back and held his wrists together, pushing them toward the alien's head. The Yollin screamed.

"Shut up!"

Lindy jammed the other one face-first into the wall. "I can't wait for you to talk to these two. They had a lot to say about how weak and worthless humans are."

Jay worked her way toward the dentist, trying not to look at the carnage.

"Who do you report to?" Rivka asked, returning her focus to the matter at hand. Images of Corranites. And another alien race. "Skaines."

She couldn't see his face because it was jammed into the floor. She expected he would start to flail as the truth was revealed.

But he didn't. "You have nothing on me because I didn't do anything wrong."

"Do you know Seequa Holmes, a dark-skinned human?" Rivka asked.

"I don't know any humans. Your race is too violent." He chuckled even with his face pressed into the short pile of the carpet. In his mind, the woman's face was clear. She was unconscious in all his memories. The Yollins were there. And some Skaines.

"Hey, Doc. Can you hold this one down for me? I need to talk to our hard-shelled friends."

Tyler studied his charge one last time; Klavin was still breathing. "Let me know if anything changes."

Jay nodded and took the dentist's place when he stood.

"Hold his wrists and keep pushing up while keeping your weight over your knee and pressed into the middle of his back. Don't let him get any leverage," Rivka instructed, letting Tyler take the perp's wrists. He straddled the Auroran, pushing hard on his back shell while keeping a tight grip on his wrists.

Rivka tipped her chin toward Red to keep his eye on the doc and Ch'ta'ka.

"Okay, buddy, I have a few questions."

"I'm saying nothing. I want my barrister!"

"You want your two dollars, I know. Just shut up. Stop clacking your mandibles, too. They're pissing me off." She leaned close and whispered, "What is your relationship to the High Chancellor?"

Images of a gathering where the High Chancellor was being introduced to a conglomeration of aliens. She didn't see any victims. The Yollin only wanted his picture taken with the human authority. He was obliged, and carried the image in his datapad.

"Where is your datapad?" she asked.

He started to panic. Images and thoughts flooded his undisciplined mind.

"She can read your mind, you idiots! Think about sex," Ch'ta'ka grumbled as loudly as he could. The words came out muffled, but the Yollins were too vulnerable. They could think of nothing besides what she planted in their minds.

Rivka took hold of the second one. "What do you know of Seequa Holmes?" He had carried her into the shuttle and given her an additional injection to keep her unconscious. "Who gives you your orders?"

She took hold of the first Yollin. He was thinking the same as the other.

"Ch'ta'ka. You are a trafficker and a slave trader. You are guilty as sin. There is only one sentence for your crimes. You have been judged."

She put Reaper against the side of his head. "You won't

feel a thing, unfortunately, unlike your victims.

"Wait!" he cried.

"The famous last words of every scumbag when they realize that their days of crime are over."

"I'll tell you what you want to know," he pleaded.

"You already have. Where are the Skaines?" she asked quickly.

He clamped his mind down and started thinking repulsive thoughts. She punched him in the head with her free hand.

"The only leverage you have," she started, speaking softly, "is to tell me what you know. If you aren't going to tell me, you will be dead one minute from now. If you tell me, you will be alive, and I will consider commuting your sentence to life in solitary confinement on Jhiordaan."

He started to relent but was torn. The conflict within his mind was great. He was used to being in charge, so he couldn't fathom his current circumstance.

"Where. Are. The Skaines?" she whispered harshly.

He sighed and gave her the images that she was looking for. They were based out of Mecca but had gone ahead to Corran to arrange the newest contributions for the auction block.

A team of Fenek wearing white squeezed through the twisted wreckage of the doorway and placed a hover-stretcher next to Klavin. They carefully moved him. The first Fenek attended to the officer while the second hesitated when he saw the bodies.

"They're all dead," Red explained, pointing to what was left of the bodies. Point-blank railgun engagements tended to be messy. Red pointed to Ch'ta'ka and the two

Yollins. "And these three are in custody." Red stood to his full height, the railgun called Blazer balanced easily across his forearms. Lindy stood behind him, holding the Yollin in her charge by the zip ties she'd snapped around his wrists.

The attendant mumbled something and started to leave. He stopped once through the doorway. "Whoever scorched the wound probably saved his life."

"Chalk another one up for the doc," Red said. A team of officers entered as soon as the emergency services pair had left.

Rivka pointed with one hand while holding her datapad below her chin. "Please detain these three for surrender to Federation custody and transfer to Jhiordaan. They've all been found guilty of violating Federation Law, Title 4, Section 1, Sub-section 31—Trafficking in Sentient species. They've also been found guilty of other crimes like battery under this section, but also Title 5, Section 1, Crimes of Intent—Conspiracy. They are extremely violent, and are to be shackled at all times."

Rivka recited the order for Chaz to request a pickup team with a prison shuttle. The pad flashed green to show that it had been transmitted. She shoved it back in her pocket.

"Ladies and gentlemen, our work here is finished. We need to be on our way to Corran." They watched the officers secure the three. The Yollins snarled and snapped, but the Auroran assumed a look of tranquility. Rivka jumped at him, throwing a wild punch toward the side of his head, but he was already slipping down. The Fenek officer eased him to the ground.

He checked for a pulse. "He's...dead," he said, unsure of his own words.

"Committed suicide rather than be incarcerated. It appears to be the slavers' way," Rivka remarked emotionlessly. The officer looked confused. "Even though he wanted to live, in his mind. I guess the power of the Skaines compelled him."

"Don't let these two out of your sight," Rivka motioned indiscriminately toward the Yollins. She wondered if they were too low on the chain to have been implanted with the suicide solution. In the end, it didn't matter. She'd issued their death sentence. Whether it happened now or later, their days in the slave trade were over.

She puffed out her cheeks as she contemplated the team's next steps.

"This was only one cell. There are more operating out of Mecca, a place of business, culture, and recreation. And a place where you can be kidnapped and sold into slavery," she intoned as if narrating a documentary.

"What can we do about that?" Jay asked.

"Hold up," Rivka directed of the officers removing the two Yollins. One looked more belligerent than the other, although neither was pleased with getting caught. "Who do you work with here in Mecca?"

Images, locations, aliens, Fenek. She couldn't tell from the jumbled thoughts who was involved in the seedy underworld and who was active in their day-to-day lives.

"What other Yollins are slavers? Where are the Skaines located in Mecca? Are there other Aurorans involved?"

Rivka smiled. Better questions yield better answers. She tapped furiously on her datapad. "Chaz, forward that to the commissioner, please. Those are the addresses of their conspirators. To cut the heart out of this ring, raid those places and seize everyone they can find. Leave the Skaines to us. We'll take them into custody on Corran."

Red and Lindy gave her their thumbs-ups. The dentist brushed himself off and nodded. He was ready to go. Jay was already waiting at the door.

"It's time I don my barrister's robes and storm the Corran court on Ms. Holmes' behalf."

"You have robes? Is that like a cloak?" the dentist asked.

"No." Rivka shook her head. "It's a figure of speech."

"Do you have a wig?" he pressed.

"No wig."

"No trappings of power?"

She pointed to her Magistrates' jacket.

"The perps usually see that right before they get their asses kicked," Red interjected.

Tyler looked disappointed.

"Fine. I'll wear my formal attire to attend the court, but if we have to fight our way out, I shall be quite upset."

"Because it's a mission..." Red said slowly.

"Case!"

"He has a point," the dentist suggested. "If I had to fight my way out of appointments, I would have to call them something else. Maybe missions."

"And here I thought we were too busy to waste time on no-value-added endeavors." The team walked quickly through the corridors of the building on their way to *Peacekeeper*. Red watched for threats, but the presence of law enforcement had chased the locals into their homes. No one walked casually about now.

"I wonder if the commissioner and his people found anything on their raid," Jay asked.

"That's a good question, Jay." Rivka nodded toward the young woman, her flaming red hair taking on a life of its own in response to her movements. The Magistrate gazed pointedly at Red and Tyler. Her bodyguard shrugged one shoulder, unintimidated by *the look*. "I'll send a note when we're on the ship and request an update on Klavin."

They continued to the corvette without incident, and after they boarded, Chaz took the ship out.

"Next stop, Corran," Rivka told the crew. "Seequa, we're coming to get you out."

CHAPTER FIFTEEN

The Royal City of Khn'Chik on Yoll

"How do *we* fix this?" Grainger asked.

"We have at least five major initiatives ongoing simultaneously. First and foremost is Lance Reynolds' negotiations to bring Corran into the Federation. Next is an undercover operation by one of our freelance teams known as the Shadow Vanguard. There's Rivka, and then there are some localized operations. These are all coming together. I had to bide my time and hope that my failure didn't see the light of day until we could wrap the noose around the necks of those who deserve it." High Chancellor Wyatt glanced at the Magistrate before turning back to the window and watching the world go by.

"How do *we* fix this?" Grainger repeated. "Are these operations going to roll up the organization from top to bottom, cleaning up the tendrils in between?"

"Call Rivka," Wyatt directed. Grainger pulled out his datapad, but the High Chancellor waved for him to put it away.

"Yes, High Chancellor. I am connecting you now," a disembodied voice said. Wyatt turned his monitor around and took the seat next to Grainger.

"They are just returning now from their engagement in Mecca. Don't tell the Magistrate this," the AI said in a low and conspiratorial voice, "but I believe it was a resounding success. If you'll standby, please, I'll connect you."

"We surrender our secrets to our AIs," Grainger said.

"Success shouldn't be kept secret. Thanks for sharing, Chaz," Wyatt remarked.

"What did Chaz share?" Rivka asked before her face appeared on the screen.

"That your work on Mecca was successful."

"Yes, that. We didn't get shot or killed. Well, we did get shot, but the body armor protected us." Rivka said carefully, guarding her words. She was unsure of the High Chancellor, and that bothered her more than anything.

A voice off-screen added, "Tell him about the running."

"I'm not telling him about the running." She turned to face the voice and gave the international signal for cut.

"I feel like we should hear about the running," Grainger suggested.

"Oh, hey! Didn't see you there, Leibchen." Rivka frowned.

"Zombie."

"We don't have much time," the High Chancellor interrupted. "Grainger and I have talked about my appearance in this investigation. I have to apologize to you, Magistrate Anoa, for not making you aware of my unsuccessful attempt to penetrate this organization."

"Your explanation is good enough, High Chancellor. I

don't need an apology. I only need guidance on how we can fix it."

"You sound like Grainger." Wyatt smiled.

"I'm not sure if that's supposed to be a compliment." Rivka felt the weight lifted from her soul.

Grainger tried to pout but couldn't.

"Ankh? Can you find those pictures and remove them?" Rivka asked.

"Of course," the Crenellian replied, popping into half the screen.

"What about the Skaines?" Rivka wondered.

"Our long-lost cousins," Ankh said with uncharacteristic emotion. "They are the galaxy's villains. If you find a crime syndicate and dig deep enough, the dregs will reveal the footprints of Skaines. Yes. I am tracking them, but they have generations of experience in how to violate the law. They do not make it easy, but the Federation makes it possible to keep them under surveillance."

"Is it one group?" Wyatt stared at the Crenellian's face, which was still taking up half the screen.

"Yes," Ankh replied with confidence.

"How many members in the group?"

Ankh's eyes unfocused as he carried on a short conversation with the AI that lived in his head. "Erasmus says that we are looking for eight hundred and seventeen Skaines."

"I had hoped the number would be smaller," Grainger complained.

"Eight hundred of that number are on five Skaine vessels. The Bad Company's conflict resolution branch is tracking them at present."

"Terry Henry," Wyatt said. "In that case, we have seventeen scumbags who need to be collected. Do you know where they are?"

"Four are on Yoll."

The High Chancellor's eyes turned cold.

"Where?"

"Inconclusive," Ankh replied. "I'm transmitting what I have to you and Grainger."

"The other thirteen?" Rivka asked.

"Four right here in Mecca, and nine between Fenek Eudoxius and Corran."

"Is four the number that runs a cell?" Grainger asked.

"Yes. That is a complete cell. For criminals, the Skaines are well organized."

Wyatt raised one eyebrow.

"Magistrate Rivka Anoa," the High Chancellor said as if addressing the court. "I am pleased beyond measure that our paths crossed and you have joined us. We are challenged by something greater than any of us, but we contribute individually. It is thankless, and we are attacked. Today alone, your people have been shot at, and I hear there was running."

He snickered softly. Rivka glared at someone off-screen and flinched when a wombat flew into her lap. She petted Floyd's head and scratched behind her ears before turning her attention back to the screen.

"I can give you nothing except my thanks. There are no promotions. There are no benefits beyond what you already have. Peacekeeping in the galaxy is its own reward, as hollow as those words are. Never lose sight of what you are doing for those who will never know and can never appreciate the pain you've suffered on their behalf."

A tear formed and fell from the corner of Rivka's eye. Floyd nuzzled her vigorously.

"I don't know what to say."

"Keep on keeping on," Wyatt suggested.

"We could use a bigger ship," Red said from off-screen.

"Vered. Thanks for keeping the Magistrate safe," the High Chancellor replied.

"She doesn't make it easy, High Chancellor."

"I suspect she doesn't. We have impounded a couple ships, but if TH and the *War Axe* are successful, a Skaine cutter could be yours. I'll send him a note and inform Nathan Lowell. We'll see what we can do. Bad Company has a significant fleet of warships. They may be able to break one of their Harborian vessels free. In either case, we will get you a bigger ship. Are you adding more crew?"

"Ankh has locked me out of my own bridge. Hamlet is wreaking havoc, and my deck is still covered with blood since the cleaning bots can't get access because there are always people in here. I have a suit of powered combat armor lashed to the outside of the ship because there's no room in the hold."

"Sorry. I thought you had a *real* need for a bigger ship." Wyatt waited to see if he got a rise.

"Now *you* sound like Grainger," Rivka replied evenly.

"I'll see what I can do, Magistrate. Give General Reynolds a call, and make sure you dovetail with his negotiations. Bringing Corran into the Federation will be the catalyst that will send the rats scrambling to find a new trade. When they're in the open, we'll crush them."

"The Skaines will rue the day they crossed you," Rivka stated.

"I hope they do, although they don't see the error of their ways, so they'll have to grumble from within the confines of a prison. We may not defeat this generation, but we're going to put a hurt on it."

"Hear, hear!" Rivka cheered. "Gotta run. We've broken orbit and need to square some things with the commissioner before we Gate to Corran. Rivka out."

Grainger took a deep breath before standing. "There are days where I love my job more than the other days. Today is one of those days. If you'll allow it, I'd like to be a part of the Skaine take-down, which I have to assume is going to happen soon."

"Coordinate with Zai'den to join the Tac Team. If you've never seen a Yollin enforcement squad make an arrest, you're in for a treat."

"Violent?" Grainger wondered.

"You have no idea. The Skaines picked a bad day to set up shop on Yoll."

Slave Pits, Corran

"Has it been two weeks yet, Waffle Face?" Seequa Holmes shouted through the bars. "If I could reach your neck, I'd squeeze it until your ugly-ass head popped off!"

Her sole jailor kept his distance, only dropping off food when she was asleep. She had tried to fake it, but they knew. She wondered if they had inserted a monitor into her body. Too many conspiracy theories ran through her mind. She had nothing but time to think about the ways she'd been mistreated, which enraged her.

No one would buy a slave who was untamed, which

was exactly what she wanted. She had never contemplated what they would do with a slave that couldn't be sold.

"Come here!" she called in a friendly voice, crooking a finger toward the face in the distance. "Just a few words..."

The Corranite didn't move.

"I so want you to die," she mumbled as she sat down on the twin bed, the only piece of furniture in her cage.

A light appeared as a door opened next to the guard. Two more Corranites were silhouetted as they passed through and disappeared when the door closed, extinguishing the supplemental light. The guard talked to the newcomers briefly. The door opened again, and one Corranite left.

She thought it had been the guard. Seequa found herself standing at the bars, staring into the darkness at the far end of the area where the incorrigible slaves were held. There were a couple other aliens she couldn't identify and was incapable of talking with. She was the most alone she'd ever been in her life.

All because of that asshole Callius Markmal. Her lip quivered, and she clenched her fists so tightly that her fingernails started to cut into her palms. The beast within her growled as she worked herself into a furor, but it quickly passed. She was weak from lack of food. They were systematically starving her into compliance.

She grabbed the bars and tried to shake them, but they didn't budge or rattle.

"Never!" she screamed.

The two Corranites approached. "You don't wish to be freed?" one asked.

"What?" she asked, the being's words not registering.

The second Corranite unlocked the cage and opened the door. "You're free to go, but I must warn you not to break the law. Otherwise, no one will be able to save you."

"Where's my stuff?" she asked.

"This is all you have." The alien pointed at her dirty prison garb. She didn't even have shoes. She had no identification. She had no money. She had nothing but the clothes on her back.

"You pieces of shit! You take everything I own and dump me on the street and then tell me not to commit a fucking crime on this shithole third world when I don't even know where I am? Is there a Federation Embassy?"

"There is not. Corran, where you are, is not a member of the Federation."

"You pack of fucks!" She thought about remaining in the cage, but she'd had enough of that. She was street-smart; she'd figure it out, but from the outside, not the inside. "Can you let my lawyer know?"

"Know what?"

"That you suck hairy bistok balls." She finally let go of the bars and flexed her hands. She took a tentative step, and then another. When she was outside the cage, she studied her captors. Or maybe they were her liberators.

"In the city proper, such verbal attacks will get you thrown in a real prison. This place is a palace by comparison," the Corranite explained, gesturing toward the doorway.

"I know, fuckstick—don't let the door hit me in the ass on the way out. You fucking people suck. Your whole race sucks. I bet when I get outside, I'm going to find that your fucking planet sucks." She flipped them the double bird as she stormed toward the door. As much as she wanted to wring her guard's neck, she didn't want to spend another minute in a cage.

She stumbled through the darkness until she found the door, then yanked it open and walked into the light of the main floor, where other slaves were getting outfitted with basic necessities. She looked at the various booths, seeing all manner of things she could use in her current state of penury.

But the cage...

With her head held high, she started to climb toward the exit. "Fuck all y'all."

CHAPTER SIXTEEN

"The Corranites said I can't bring anyone else. I have to go alone."

"I am *not* good with that, Magistrate," Red complained.

"If this was a Federation planet, we'd play the trump card and bull our way through, but we don't have that luxury here. At one end of the spectrum, we get to take down major crime syndicates, and then there are times like this where one life is worth the risk. I'm putting my barrister hat on, and I'm going to defend Miss Holmes with all that I have. I won't rest until I bring her out of there."

The bodyguards shifted uncomfortably. Even though Rivka had given them the order that they were to remain behind, they had geared up and were ready to go. They wrestled with the frustration of not being able to do their job.

"Can I go with you?" Tyler asked standing to show that he was unarmed.

"No one. Not even Floyd!" Rivka tried to defuse the

tension. The wombat always loved being the center of attention. "Your job is to make everyone happy."

Wheee! Floyd shuffled around to get her head scratched by each person in succession, finishing with Rivka.

"Stay in touch," Jay said softly. She lifted Floyd into her arms, grunting from the effort. "Who's been giving her treats?"

No one would meet Jay's gaze.

Wheee!

"No! You're getting fat."

Rivka used the distraction to leave, and the whole crew watched her. Hamlet appeared and tried to use Red's leg as a scratching post.

The hatch to the bridge remained secured. The Magistrate hesitated as she walked past and reached into her pocket to ensure she had a couple of Ankh's hacking devices. They provided her a certain amount of comfort. "I want my bridge back," she told the closed door.

Rivka left the ship without another word. She didn't bother to close the hatch, knowing that her crew would take care of it.

At the aerovan, a single being waited.

Palatius Lore.

"So, we meet again," Rivka stated.

"Your trip has been wasted. It was a case of mistaken identity, and Seequa Holmes has been released.

"When? Where is she?"

"Yesterday, and I have no idea."

"Who would know?"

"I'm sure Miss Holmes would know."

"How can I get in touch with her?" Rivka's mind raced

as she interrogated the Corranite near her ship on the tarmac of the spaceport.

"I don't know. She doesn't have a Corran-based communication link."

"She doesn't have anything, does she?" The realization hit Rivka. In her study of Corranite law, she found that it was a strictly regulated society where the rules could be easily broken by the unsuspecting. *Mens rea*, or intent, was not a requisite factor in the determination of one's guilt. "You set her up to break the law, and in that case, the Federation would have no recourse where if she was sold illegally, that would be a blight on Corran."

"But she was *not* sold illegally," Palatius countered.

"No, she was not. Has the governor-general put you at my disposal?"

"Unfortunately." Palatius didn't lie. It would have been too easy to disprove.

"Then we shall use the transportation the government has graciously provided to find Miss Holmes. Please, we need to hurry. I think we should start at the main trade hall."

The Magistrate couldn't read the emotions on the Corranite's face but suspected he was fuming. She decided to blow a little methane into the fire.

"And if we see any Skaines, I'd like to stop and talk to them."

"They are protected as guests on Corran," he shot back.

"As am I, Palatius." Rivka smiled pleasantly. "Shall we?"

He gave instructions to the aerovan and it took off, heading for Amberly's city center.

. . .

The Royal City of Khn'Chik on Yoll

Grainger disappeared behind the hulking forms of the armed and armored Yollin tac team.

They approached from the building's blind side, and two teammates peeled off to cover the rear exit. They were armed with big pistols shaped to fit the larger Yollin hands and stun batons, and they expected the Skaines to be armed, maybe with railguns or plasma rifles.

The tac team had surprise on their side. Four drones hovered overhead, using infrared, ultraviolet, and millimeter wave scans to track the suspects' locations within the building. The Skaines appeared to be relaxed and unsuspecting.

But they were Skaines, a distrustful bunch with small, skinny blue bodies and oversized heads. Many considered them to be evil. Others thought their base culture was incompatible with most societies. Different, not evil.

Regardless, they caused the Federation a significant amount of pain and anguish since their proclivities diametrically opposed good order and discipline. They thrived on the chaos of crime.

In their circles, they had a hierarchy that made sense, an honor code to which they adhered but did not apply to aliens. Or Skaines they didn't like.

Grainger followed the team to the front door. Their heavy carapaces seemed thicker than those of normal Yollins. A pistol in one hand and a stun baton in the other, the breach leader prepared to blast the door. A quick hand-scan showed it to be barred.

The Yollin laughed at the effort as he placed shaped

demolitions that would rip out the entire doorframe. The bar would fall uselessly to the floor. They checked the locations of the Skaines inside and searched at close range for any spring traps, weapons that would activate automatically.

The active scans didn't find weapons, but they discovered that the floor was tied into the power circuit.

"Ready?" the breach leader asked. The team clacked their mandibles, keeping their hands on their weapons. They tensed as they prepared to follow the explosive blast through the door. "Cut the power."

The lights went out, and the floor ceased pulsing. The explosion ripped out the doorframe, and the first Yollin was so close behind it that he stepped on it before it hit the floor. The team fanned into the room, racing for the Skaines.

The suspects were almost as quick to take action as the tac team.

Almost. A railgun barked, and a hypervelocity round burst through an interior wall on its way through the exterior wall to somewhere beyond. The Yollins returned fire, silencing the weapon. A harsh voice shouted, followed by the thud of a body hitting the floor. Grainger remained near the entry, securing it against escape while waiting for the action to end.

"One target on the roof," a team member reported. Two Yollins had already gone upstairs, and they now turned their attention upward before clearing the floor. A pair raced from the ground floor to backstop them. Grainger checked the feed on his datapad. One Skaine was down, one was detained, and one was holed up in a panic room.

The last had made it to the roof and was under observation by a drone.

The Skaine spotted it, calmly took aim, and downed the craft. The tac team ran onto the roof before the suspect could reorient and hit him with the stun clubs—, probably more times than was necessary since he dropped the plasma rifle after the first baton engaged.

One team member picked up the unconscious Skaine and slung him over his shoulder, the other quickly secured his hands and feet before picking up the plasma rifle and joining his partner as they returned downstairs.

"Two captured, one dead, and one holed up in a panic room that is secured by warship-grade materials. We don't have anything to breach it," the leader reported.

A voice replied over the general comm. "Use the railgun to kill him before he destroys any evidence, and we'll burn it open at our leisure."

Using the various scan systems available to him, the breach leader found a gap between the plates. He marked the spot on the wall with his fingernail. He pointed and held the scanner at eye level. The team member with the Skaine railgun aimed at the point on the wall and waited. The leader adjusted his aim. "Steady," he said. "Fire."

The single hypervelocity tungsten flechette thundered from the rail and through the wall. When the dust cleared, the leader nodded. "Suspect is neutralized."

He tapped the wall where the door was, and the team collected near the entry point. Grainger joined them. The breach leader pointed to the two Skaines in custody. "They're all yours, Magistrate."

"Nice work, Skipper. Secure all electronics for study."

Grainger turned back to the suspects. One was still unconscious, but he would wake up. "Well, my little friends, let's see what you can tell me about the trafficking business..."

The support facility was exactly as Rivka remembered it. The slow bustle of activity greeted her, and a distinct lack of urgency marked the movements of those dressed in slave attire. Rivka stopped the first person she saw. "Have you seen a dark-skinned human woman?"

"What's that?" the four-eyed alien asked before moving on. Palatius laughed. Rivka ignored him.

I'm at the main trade hall, she relayed to the crew. *Seequa is running free somewhere around the city. She was released yesterday, and we have to find her before she inadvertently commits a crime.*

As you've already told us once, Ankh replied. *I'm working on it, but the Corranites have a robust security system. It could be a while before Erasmus and I are able to penetrate it. Have you considered looking around?*

Rivka tried to look pleasant to the outside world, but her cheeks flexed as she gritted her teeth. *Find me Seequa Holmes. Rivka out.*

The Magistrate walked across the floor asking everyone she met, touching them as she went. "...dark-skinned human..."

She strolled by a number of them, and one mind flashed an image of the human. Rivka jumped backward, trying to find who it was. She wrestled briefly with a towering creature, but it wasn't him. She moved past and through a mob. "You saw the human?"

The small alien was trying to hide in the shadows of the others. Rivka hadn't touched her at all, which led to the confusion. The alien radiated empathy. The Magistrate knelt and crouched to be eye to eye. "I feel you," she told the small creature, bowing her head.

"I feel you," the alien replied.

"The human. I must find her."

"She left by that door wearing nothing but her prison garb. No shoes. No goods." A small hand pointed toward one of the exits.

"Thank you. May you find the peace you seek," Rivka said, feeling it was the right thing to say.

"Not here, but I will find it," the alien replied.

Rivka stood and strode briskly for the exit. Palatius called for her to slow down, but she shouted back at him to hurry up. She bolted through the door, immediately stopping to get her bearings. "Where would you go from here?" Rivka asked aloud, trying to put herself in Seequa's place.

The Magistrate looked at the single walkway that went to a nearby transit nexus. Without money or ID, she wouldn't be able to take private transportation.

"Do your public buses cost anything?"

"No," Palatius replied.

"Do you need identification to ride?" Rivka quickly clarified, glaring at her escort.

"Yes," the Corranite answered.

Rivka wanted to pound him into last week but restrained herself. "Malicious compliance, huh? If that's how you want to play it, fine. Let me tell you a secret: I know for a fact that you were in on the attempted coup. You were the one who gave the shooters access, and you're planning to do it again but better."

The Corranite remained frozen, the expression on his fibrous face not changing.

"All I want is the woman, and then I'm leaving. The longer this takes, the longer I'll be here, and if anything happens to her, I will debrief directly with the governor-general. That's not a threat; that's our standard operating procedure when a human life is in jeopardy. So, you can help me, or to be blunt, fuck you."

He took a step forward and Reaper appeared in her hand. She aimed at the center mass of the creature looming over her.

"Is that a weapon?" Palatius asked.

"You took away my bodyguards, but you can't remove my ability to protect myself. Being unarmed is an invitation to be a victim. I'm nobody's victim. You will die, Palatius Lore, but do you want it to be today?"

CHAPTER SEVENTEEN

The Bad Company's Conflict Resolution Command Ship
War Axe

"Run, you bastards! You'll just die with your tanks empty!" Colonel Terry Henry Walton howled from the command deck of the destroyer *War Axe*.

"What's gotten into him?" Captain Micky San Marino asked from the comfort of his chair, which dominated the bridge. The crew worked their positions as professionals. Helm and Systems managed the intricacies of the ship during a combat operation, but they were back-stopped by the team within the Combat Operations Center. It was buried deep within the ship and protected by layers of bulkheads and redundancies.

Micky considered himself to be old-school. He liked being on the bridge, mounted above the superstructure, using his eyes to see his enemy yet trusting his systems, along with the ship's AI, to do the right things.

"He's been watching too many old movies. I swear, he's

seen them all before, but watching them fresh after a hundred and fifty years makes him act weird."

"You pronounced 'young at heart' wrong," Terry interjected.

"Of course. That's what I meant." Charumati, his were-wolf partner, rolled her eyes and shook her head but snaked an arm around his waist. He reciprocated, and the two stood there as one, each a perfect balance to the other.

"Are we going to have to destroy it?" Terry asked earnestly.

"Standby, Colonel Walton," General Smedley Butler, the AI, relayed over the bridge's speakers.

Terry looked at the captain, but he didn't know.

"Prepare to fire the main guns at these coordinates." Smedley projected the tactical situation on the main screen. The last two Skaine ships in the small convoy were closing on each other as they raced to escape the *War Axe's* interdiction. A blinking light appeared at a point in between the converging tracks.

"Why are they coming together? Shouldn't they be going in opposite directions?" Terry asked.

"If they weren't trying to consolidate their firepower for a single strike, maybe. But they're Skaines. Forget everything you know about tactics. Whereas we would go separate directions to give one of the two a chance at survival," Smedley explained, "the Skaines don't trust each other. Risking themselves to save their fellows defies logic. We're going to use it against them. Fire the mains and launch the missile."

The massive guns sent a dual stream of superheated plasma at near-light speed while a single missile ejected from a launch tube and fired downrange at a seemingly casual pace compared to the plasma.

"I love the sight of that," Terry said, twisting his head to see past the main screen image to the screen showing the exterior view. Like a stream of fire, the plasma painted a line into the void.

"Wait for it," Smedley offered with panache.

"Better get your people ready, TH. Prepare to board the Skaine vessels."

"Roger that, Skipper. We've been cooling our heels too long, watching others fight and then cleaning up the mess they leave behind. It's time to kick some scumbag ass." Terry and Char hurried from the bridge.

"It's admirable when people love their jobs," the captain said to no one in particular.

"Bullseye!" Smedley exclaimed. The stream of plasma projectiles scorched both ships as they closed and jockeyed in an attempt to maneuver the other ship into the line of fire. The missile detonated, sending a targeted electromagnetic pulse over both ships.

Systems failed, and the ships floated on ballistic trajectories.

"Get in front of those ships and secure them. Bring the cutter into the hangar bay. Secure the other outside the gravitic shields." Micky leaned back in his chair, a smile slowly creeping across his face. "Nice shooting, Smedley. All hands, this is the captain. We're bringing the Skaines aboard. Watch those evil little bastards. Secure first and ask questions later."

.   .   .

The Royal City of Khn'Chik on Yoll

Grainger glared across the table at the big blue head. He wasn't much taller than a child, and looked like one sitting in an interrogation chair made for a two-legged Yollin. Grainger felt small in the chair, but at least his feet touched the floor. The Skaine's legs were shackled and hooked to the immovable chair, and his wrists were clamped to the table. He looked contorted and uncomfortable.

And also hostile.

"I don't know why we're here. You're guilty, and we're sending you and your buddy into the nearest star."

"The Etheric Federation..." the Skaine spat. "Murdering honest citizens. So much for your talk of freedom."

"Interesting." Grainger leaned his elbows on the table. The blue creature yanked on his chains, but the effort was weak. Physical intimidation wasn't the small alien's strong suit. The Magistrate didn't even flinch. "Information could buy you a reprieve from your death sentence."

"You want me to be like you? Mistrustful and dishonest?" The Skaine peered at the human before continuing, "I'd rather die with my dignity intact."

Grainger laughed to the point of shaking. His eyes watered, and when he was finally able to talk, he stammered, "I thought you were Skaine. You'd sell your own sister for a credit. You'd sell out your whole race for ten."

The creature yanked on his chains again, then slumped from overexertion.

"Tell me about the slave trade. I need the names of your suppliers. Who acquired the sentient capital in which you traded?"

"We don't trade in sentient beings. That would be illegal." The smirk on the Skaine's face suggested he thought he was funny.

"As you wish," Grainger said. "I, Magistrate Grainger, sentence you to death. Your sentence will be carried out later today when you and your twin brother are loaded into an obsolete torpedo and fired into the system's star. The good news is that most don't survive the trip. You'll be dead well before your body is burned to a crisp. I don't know who you're willing to die to protect, but that is the only thing that matters that I've gotten from our *conversation*."

Grainger stood, turned, and opened the door. He took one step through.

"Wait," the Skaine said.

"Ten seconds," Grainger growled, crossing his arms and leaning against the doorframe.

"The others were running the operation."

"Death it is," Grainger said and closed the door. The Skaine's incoherent screams beat against the inside of the door.

The Magistrate pointed to the next door, and a guard opened it. The Skaine in this room still had a twitch from being stunned into unconsciousness. He'd received enough juice to light a small city. Grainger was surprised he was still alive.

"That dumbass across the hall said you and the others were running the operation."

"It's our way," the Skaine said in a small and tired voice, conceding while admitting nothing.

"You know what the punishment is for the crime of slave trading."

"I know, but we don't care about your Federation laws. They have no bearing on what we do."

Grainger smiled, steepling his fingers before him. "But they do. The rest of your life will be spent under the burden of punishment for violation of the very laws that you flout."

"Center of the target, Magistrate. My compliments," the Skaine replied before his eye started to twitch anew.

"You're different from any other Skaine I've had the displeasure of speaking with."

"I've been around Federation limp dicks for too long. Your flaccidity rubs off, most unfortunately."

"Arrogance and name-calling couched within a subtle truth. You're playing chess while the others are playing kick the can." Grainger leaned back and reshaped his approach. "What do you offer in exchange for your life?"

"Never bid against yourself," the Skaine replied. "What do *you* want, and what are *you* willing to offer for it?"

"I want your suppliers, the ones who provided the sentient life forms you then put on the Corranite auction block."

"A shame that you presume my complicity in such a heinous crime."

"Offering you a life of imprisonment instead of joining scrotum-head across the hall on a one-way trip into Yoll's chromosphere is probably less than enticing. How about your freedom, as in, we ship your ass back to Skaine space?"

"There might be value in that, if I wanted to be a pariah. That's not how I want to spend my future, unless I have a ship with a crew. Then we can fly into space and leave judgment behind."

"There will be no ship and no crew." Grainger began to wonder why he bothered attempting to interrogate Skaine suspects. "What are those other three to you? Your cells usually have four, so we found four. I would think there'd be a connection to hold you together. Why is that guy willing to die before giving up any information? That is not very Skaine-like."

"I try not to waste brain cells on what the others will or won't do, but I'll play. Those three are brothers, or were. You reference just one. What happened to the other two?"

"One died an ugly death after taking potshots at us with a railgun. The other died an ugly death after barricading himself inside that industrial-strength panic room. Only you two survived to receive your death sentences."

"One brave Skaine and one coward. I expected as much. How did you capture the other? What is his name?"

"I don't know his name. I called him 'Hey!' or 'fuck-stick.'" Grainger chewed the inside of his lip as he contemplated where they were in the game. Pawns out, no bold moves. "He was incapable of adjusting his aim quickly enough from the drone to the Yollins who were after him. He killed the drone with one shot, but then the tac team was on him and took his weapon. It was then used to penetrate the panic room's barrier."

"A railgun should not have been able to defeat the armor plate."

"Didn't have to. There were gaps between the seams."

"The welding was substandard. Shame." The Skaine looked like he wanted to continue but stopped.

Grainger waited, letting the silence create the discomfort that a usual suspect would then seek to fill. But this Skaine wasn't a usual suspect. He sat silently, not fighting his shackles or cuffs.

"I doubt you have anything we want. Besides freedom without strings, I am not willing to give you anything else. Even that may be too much. If you'll excuse me, I have to be anywhere other than here."

Grainger made to stand, and already the Skaine was smiling. "You need me, and you know it."

"I'm pretty sure I don't," Grainger smiled back. "You have a great day. It's your last one."

"Vaidyn," the Skaine said softly but clearly.

"Who would that be?" Grainger stood at the door, leaning against it rather than opening it. He crossed his arms and watched the perp for other clues that might tell him what he was thinking.

"The one you're looking for. If you could undo these, I'll be on my way."

"Once verified, we'll conduct a formal transfer to someplace that's not here and less susceptible to your machinations."

"A moon on the far side of Hades?"

"Something like that. Your sentence is currently in a stay, pending further review. Let me check on this Vaidyn and see what comes up."

Amberly on Corran

"I think we should explore the riverwalk," Palatius said. Rivka held up her hands. The Corranite pointed.

"That's more like it. Thank you," she told him, but he only grunted in response. She didn't expect to convert him through common decency and good manners. Her goal was to retain her own humanity in spite of alien miscreants like Palatius Lore, because there were good ones like Ignacio Mar who deserved to be treated with dignity and respect.

Rivka set a blistering pace, taxing her nanocytes to give her all they had. She wanted Palatius to suffer by trying to keep up. When she looked back, he was nowhere to be seen. She snorted and continued to sprint in the direction the Corranite had pointed. She could see bridges and expected they crossed the as-yet-unseen river.

The climate was controlled, which made it pleasant all the time, but a human would seek shelter. Rivka wondered if Seequa knew what planet she was on. The Magistrate slowed when a walking trail appeared beyond a wall of hedges. She vaulted the well-manicured greenery and looked up and down the path, again trying to figure where a distraught human with no credits and no ID would go.

A hum made her look up. An aerovan was descending. It hovered next to the trail, and the door popped open. "Work smarter, not harder," Palatius Lore told her, beckoning her to join him.

She climbed in without comment, plastering her face against the window so she could see the various personalities walking the trail. Most of them were Corranites. Rivka knocked on the window to get their attention and Palatius grabbed her wrist. She turned on him, ready to strike, but his thoughts were focused on helping to find the woman.

"Attention," he said, and the pair stopped to face the

vehicle. "Have you seen a human on this trail wearing servant garb?"

They both pointed down the trail. The aerovan lifted off and followed the walk, slowing as it approached a bridge. It hovered on one side so they could look, but no one was underneath or in the shadows. The aerovan went over the bridge and continued to the next one.

Rivka sighed in relief as she saw the human's outline, but something didn't look right.

CHAPTER EIGHTEEN

The Royal City of Khn'Chik on Yoll

High Chancellor Wyatt looked out of place. It wasn't the nicest part of town, and the people milled about, casting furtive glances his way. Grainger stood easily at his side, basking in the radiance of the older man's presence.

"I'm glad you had nothing to do with the trade," Grainger told him softly.

"Slavers disgust me much more than murderers. They steal someone's life over and over. Every day that person remains the property of another is another day of torment. Are they worth that much? The answer is yes, because there are those like the Skaines who readily sell any other race. I'm forwarding a proposition making trading with the Skaines illegal. Making any arrangements with the Skaines illegal. Making it illegal to *be* Skaine."

"Do you think it'll fly?" Grainger replied skeptically.

"No, but we need to put them on notice. They are the galaxy's criminals. If you see a Skaine, you can guarantee that he's up to no good."

"What are we doing down here?" Grainger asked.

"Vaidyn." The High Chancellor stood patiently to the side of the thoroughfare. "There's a link down here, although the individual associated with that name isn't. It's a bizarre corkscrew of associations. We need to talk to one Malagor Beauregard."

Grainger stifled a laugh. "There's a dude named Malagor Beauregard who lives on Yoll?"

"Dudette, as it turns out. She's from a race of amorphous creatures."

"And she has information that could lead us to Vaidyn?" Grainger asked.

"That is my hope. She's associated with both Yollins and Skaines, if our search through the dark web carries any weight."

"This is where Rivka has an advantage by having Ankh on her team."

"He has been an incredible asset. Where do you think I got this information?"

"From your people?" Grainger asked naively. "You're the High Chancellor. You have to have people sitting around, ready to do your bidding. You know, people…"

Grainger's voice trailed off when he saw the bemused look on the High Chancellor's face.

"Zai'den. He's the only people I have. Well, you Magistrates and some others, but you're doing your own jobs. I'll let you in on a little secret. I answer to more people than those who answer to me."

"Ain't that some shit?" Grainger blurted.

"It is. Shall we?" The High Chancellor didn't wait for an answer. He started walking toward a small shop. He strode with the dignity and authority of his office, clearing the casual passersby from his path. He didn't have to say anything.

He commanded Grainger's respect. There was no end to thankless jobs.

"I appreciate what you do, High Chancellor, and I thank you for taking care of the other Magistrates and me."

Wyatt acknowledged the statement with a nod.

"Are you going to give Rivka a bigger ship?"

"Ship envy, Magistrate?" The High Chancellor chuckled briefly before restoring his game face.

They stepped through the door into the shop. Wyatt looked around before maneuvering his way through the crowded aisles. He squeezed past the counter, nodding his chin toward the Yollin near the payment desk.

"You can't go back there. Staff only," the clerk stated as if he'd said the same phrase a thousand times. Wyatt and Grainger ignored him. The Yollin made no other attempt to stop them.

"Miss Beauregard, I presume?" the High Chancellor said pleasantly. He stopped before a squarish plastic couch upon which a blob-like creature undulated, shimmering in the light from the room's glowing panels. "I think you know who I am and why I'm here."

"I care not for the affairs of humans," a female voice announced through a translation device on a small table beside the couch.

"But trafficking them is okay?"

"Illegal. No do."

"The Skaines, Miss Beauregard. You should have

known that no good could come from an association with Skaines."

"No association," the creature countered. The undulations rippled more quickly across the pale silvery surface of the amorphous blob. The creature started to shift and solidify and assumed the shape of a small humanoid, skinny body topped by an oversized head.

Grainger studied the creature, stepping to the side as it made its transition. Wyatt caught his arm before he moved too far away.

"Now go. Shop to run." The creature assumed a smooth gait as she headed for the room's lone door. Wyatt and Grainger stood in the way.

"I'm sorry. We didn't bring security personnel since we have no intention of apprehending you. I only want answers regarding Vaidyn. Where do we find him?"

"No idea."

"Maybe we *will* have to take you into custody then. You do know. We know you know, and now you know that we know it."

Grainger raised one eyebrow at the High Chancellor's quip.

The creature surged forward, trying to squeeze between the two men. Grainger swung an arm block, but it hit as if entering gel. He stopped with his arm embedded in what passed for the creature's upper torso and struggled to pull it free.

The High Chancellor pulled a device from his pocket and zapped Beauregard, causing her to dissolve into a puddle. He casually walked to the desk and found a container that looked to be for hot beverages. He put it in the middle of the puddle and pressed a button on its side, and it sucked Malagor Beauregard in. He flipped the lid closed and looked at Grainger, who was staring at his arm.

"What just happened?" he asked. No residue remained on his arm, but it continued to tingle.

"The Parmecium are like blowfish. They aren't very big but expand to seem more intimidating. A small electric shock renders them harmless. I built this myself from a child's toy." He shook his small device, showing two bare wires sticking out. "And they always have their travel container nearby. Shall we?"

Grainger followed Wyatt's gesture and started to walk out. "You could have told me, High Chancellor."

"After my earlier missteps, I needed to do something to regain my mystique."

"If she's so weak, why is she mixed up in the slave trade?" Grainger looked from the bored clerk to the High Chancellor.

"She's not weak. She's vulnerable. There's a difference," Wyatt explained. "If we hadn't known, then we would not have been able to stop her."

"I understand," Grainger conceded. "What do you think she'll tell us?"

"That is a good question. I hope we get an answer to it."

Christina Lowell watched from within her mechanized combat armor. A dozen similarly outfitted warriors stood in three ranks of four before the open door to *War Axe's* hangar bay.

Terry Henry and Char wore their ballistic vests and helmets, but they weren't heading into space like Christina and her team.

"When I give the order to push off, we are going to maneuver through space to the enemy cruiser. We will breach at three points, as shown on your heads up displays, where we will install the gas canisters to knock out the crew. Once confirmed, we will leave our suits in the airlocks. The Skaines are a smaller race, with ships that won't support the bulk of these beasts. So we go in lean and trim. Rules of engagement dictate that we give them a chance to surrender, but if they fire, you are authorized to use deadly force. We will neutralize all Skaines and secure the ship for impound. Questions?"

No one had any. Each fireteam of four took one massive silver cylinder and pushed through the forcefield, activating their jets to launch into space. The Skaine cruiser drifted in the distance. Christina saluted Colonel Walton, who returned her gesture with the crisp Marine Corps salute of old.

She snarled, and her eyes took on the pale yellow of the Pricolici within. She ran toward the barrier and threw herself into space. Her jets activated once outside, and she raced to get in front of her squad.

With the cruiser team out of the way, the *War Axe* maneuvered to bring the Skaine cutter, the smaller of the two ships, into the hangar bay. Armed and ready Bad Company warriors lined the sides of the space. TH dialed his Jean Dukes Special back to two. Char let her hands caress her two pistols, her constant companions all these years. They were cleaned, loaded, and ready for close combat.

"Same ROE," Terry bellowed in the great space of the hangar. He and Char hurried to the bulkhead and grabbed on as the *War Axe* approached the cutter rose on. The destroyer would wrap itself around the Skaine ship and let it set gently to the deck. Once he had verified that the warriors were hanging on, Terry gave the order. "Smedley, you can remove the gravity and bring her in."

The Bad Company became weightless as the *War Axe* moved forward. A sharp nose appeared through the forcefield, and the rest of the ship followed.

"Think she'll notice the scorch mark?" Char asked, biting her lip.

"Nah! You can barely see it. That's a nice-looking ship. Did they say why the Magistrate needed a bigger ship?"

From the nose to the tail on this side of the ship, an ugly black streak raged. Some of the hull's metal had started to peel back. It was difficult to tell the ship's original color.

"I think I heard the name 'Ankh,'" Char answered.

"She's going to need a bigger crew, too. I heard Micky talking to some people. "Are you ready, my lover?"

"Always."

The gravity was slowly restored, settling the cutter onto the deck. It canted slightly since it sat on its superstructure. The Skaines hadn't extended the landing gear.

"They want it the hard way, people. Let's give them what they asked for. Canisters up!"

One pair from each side hustled forward, rolling a canister between them. When they reached the hull, they took a number of quick soundings before finding their spots. They attached the hoses to spear-looking projectiles and fired them to create a breach to the interior. After they pressed one button, the gas started to flow, being forced through the opening at such high pressure that anyone attempting to hold it back could lose an arm. It also flooded the interior that much more quickly.

"Hoods!" he called, and they pulled their built-in helmets over their heads. Their shipsuits would be their environmental protection until the ship's air could be flushed. The teams moved into place, with Terry and Char closest to the hatch. "Open it up, Smedley."

The warship's AI responded by popping the airlock seal. Gas visibly escaped as the hatch unlocked and slowly disappeared sideways into the hull. Terry ducked his head for a quick look, pulling himself back out before anyone could aim and fire. He reached around the opening and jammed a button.

After the interior airlock door opened, TH counted down from three to zero on his fingers. When he hit one, he tensed, crouched, and bolted through the hatch on the next count. Char was right behind him as he dove through the interior hatch, but before she could reach it, laser beams cut back and forth across the space the colonel had just gone through.

Char pulled out a grenade and flung it through the opening, making it bounce down the corridor. TH did the same from his prone position in a small alcove. Char readied a second grenade and threw it after Terry's, but with much more force. He launched himself like a torpedo back into the airlock, clearing the corridor as Char's first grenade exploded, then his and her second. He was on his feet and running while the smoke was still heavy in the air.

He went right, and Char went left, and the warriors filed in behind them. The JDS barked again and again as TH single-handedly assaulted the corridor's defenders. He backed up and chucked another grenade.

Toward the front of the ship, Char fired her pistol, the old-style cartridge explosions echoing through the corridor. For a single moment, the attack went quiet. For a whole second, there was peace.

Then the grenade exploded.

CHAPTER NINETEEN

Amberly on Corran

Rivka hammered on the window as the aerovan descended at an agonizingly slow pace. Seequa Holmes was surrounded by Corranites. She swung a branch back and forth to hold them off.

"Violating the carefully manicured foliage is a crime in this city," Palatius intoned.

"Of course, it is. Your single greatest priority is getting me down there before she hurts anyone. What is the penalty for threatening someone? Culpability is on both sides." Rivka stood in the space between the seats, preparing herself in case she needed to kick her escort in the face. With a short word, the vehicle lurched and dropped the rest of the way to the ground. Rivka's reflexes kicked in and she maintained her balance. "Thank you."

She popped the door and ran into the group, bumping the locals out of the way to stop before the human. "Come with me. I'm taking you home."

"Took you long enough, bitch!" Seequa roared.

Rivka glared at the Corranites until Palatius Lore appeared. One look at him, and they made themselves scarce.

Rivka turned back to the woman. "It couldn't be avoided. There's a lot going on out there to impede progress. You're a survivor, Seequa, and you've made it. Now it's time to go home. I don't know if this will make you feel better, but of the group that kidnapped you, two are dead, and the other two are on their way to Jhiordaan. It also cracked the case to help us find the leaders and other cells. Thanks to you, we're tearing the heart out of this operation."

Seequa looked confused as she tried to parse what the Magistrate was telling her. She lifted the branch and threatened Palatius. Rivka stepped between them.

"Put it down and let's go home."

"That is a crime," Palatius said slowly.

"So is orchestrating a coup," Rivka shot back. "How about you fuck yourself?"

"Yeah!" Seequa jutted her chest and chin in his direction. "Go fuck yourself, you fucking piece-of-shit asshole!"

Rivka grabbed the woman to keep her from losing control.

"Don't talk to us," Rivka told their escort as she guided the woman toward the aerovan. Palatius followed, anger steaming from his fibrous pores.

The Skaine cutter on board the *War Axe*

"Come out with your hands up!" Terry called into the last occupied space on the cutter.

The Skaines didn't bother to reply.

"You're only going to die," Terry suggested. He looked at the remaining grenade on his belt, but it was the engine compartment. He had to be more precise in his targeting. He turned to the team. "Two high, two low. I'll take center. Hit your targets. No collateral damage. This thing needs to fly after we're done with it."

Terry checked his JDS to make sure it was still set on two, then looked at it for a moment and dialed it back to one. He counted down on his fingers, and when he finished, he charged into the engine room, snap-firing at one target before rolling. The other four were through the door in the space of a heartbeat, firing at the distracted Skaines, who now had more targets than they could engage.

Char leaned around the doorframe, picked a target amid the chaos, and ended him. Then a second one. TH low-crawled toward a coolant pump. The firing stopped, and the team to the left yelled, 'Clear.' The team to the right did the same. Char walked into the middle of the space, aiming steadily over her husband.

He reached the complex tangle of pump and pipes, poked his JDS in between, and pulled the trigger. The top of a Skaine head appeared as the creature tried to jump out of the way. Char fired.

The body slumped to the deck, evidence of Char's accuracy painted across the tank behind where he stood.

Terry stood and brushed himself off. "Nice shot," he told her with a smile. Terry held a finger to his head as he communed with all parties inside the cutter before reporting, "The ship is secure, and we took no injuries."

"You don't need to do that," Char said, pointing to the finger alongside his temple.

"I really do," he replied before quickly taking his hand away.

"No injuries?" Char pointed to his shoulder, where a laser had struck. The bleeding had already stopped.

"Just a flesh wound," he countered.

"You don't have to go first." She pulled his uniform jacket away to examine the injury and nodded once, comfortable that it wasn't worse than he was admitting.

"I can't order people to do something I wouldn't."

"They all know you would, because you have. For decades, you have. As the Bad Company takes on greater roles, we need more *like* you, not more *from* you."

"How did I marry so well?" he said, but his face was serious. He had been contemplating that very thing, but preferred the individual actions like clearing the ship over the strategic actions of building a fleet from the Harborian vessels, crewing them, and conducting interdictions across the galaxy. That was making him feel old.

"Because I settled for what was available in a sparse world." Char's purple eyes sparkled as she needled her partner.

"We tried to retire once, and it bored the snot out of us." Terry stood close to her and reached out, but winced when he flexed his shoulder. He started rotating it gently to keep it limber.

"It bored the snot out of *you*."

"It did. I'm not ready for round two, but maybe it's time for I & I duty."

"'I and I?'" Char hadn't heard the expression before.

"It's from the Marines. Inspector Instructor. Active-duty Marines check on the reserves to make sure they are doing what they need to remain prepared in case they're called up."

"Yes. You should try that. *We* should do that." She pointed to his shoulder. "That could have been your head."

"With the size of this melon, you're not kidding!" Terry quipped, wrapping his good arm around Char's waist. "We better get this ship cleaned up before turning it over to the legal beagles." Terry hesitated. "I wonder why the gas didn't work? As in, I wonder how Christina is faring?"

His finger returned to his temple as he made to contact her.

The gas didn't work? Christina asked since her teams had breached and had the canisters in place but were not yet pumping their knock-out gas into the interior of the Skaine cruiser.

They were ready for us. I wonder if we let it linger long enough. We pumped the gas in and hit the hatch about twenty seconds later.

We'll give it five minutes. It's supposed to leave them unconscious for a good hour. I don't have enough firepower to take down a cruiser. If we fit in the corridor in our suits, it'd be no problem, but we don't. Thirteen of us, and roughly a hundred of them? I can't risk it, Terry.

I concur, Terry told her. *Don't risk your people. These bastards tried to put up a good fight, but we only had to contend with a quarter of your number.*

Roger. Will advise. She closed the link and switched to the suit to suit comm. "Listen up, people. We deliver the gas, wait five minutes, and then hit them hard. First team, hard-breach the hold, and Teams Two and Three, override the airlocks and enter. Don't de-suit until we're sure they're out cold."

"We won't fit through the airlock in our suits," Private Gefelton remarked from Team Two.

"Team one will be our eyes and ears. Be ready to access the airlocks on my command. Give them a breath of fresh air, courtesy of the Bad Company. Execute."

A chorus of "Aye, aye, ma'am," confirmed her order. She watched Team Two open the valve and start pumping the gas into the Skaine ship.

"Countdown of five minutes, please," she told her HUD. A timer displayed and started the glacially slow march of watched time.

Amberly on Corran

Seequa nearly collapsed into the seat inside the aerovan. Rivka hovered protectively over her, making sure her body acted as a barrier between the woman and the Corranite.

Palatius took his seat and issued the commands for the aerovan to take them to *Peacekeeper*. Rivka didn't argue. The vehicle shifted, and she almost fell. She glared at Palatius Lore as if he'd done it on purpose. The aerovan bumped again and she stumbled, purposefully falling onto the Corranite.

"When's the coup?" she asked, her face a mere hand's

breadth from his. Flashes of violence. Pure raging hatred. The governor-general in a pool of his own blood.

With Rivka right next to him, his thoughts calmed as quickly as they raged.

"I think it best you leave Corran as soon as possible. I will clear the airspace for you to leave the second you are back on board."

"I appreciate that. Thanks for your help. I hope this is the last time I am ever on Corran," she lied smoothly.

I'll be back, and I'm bringing the pain.

She turned to Seequa, who stared out the window with unseeing eyes.

"We'll get you some good food and a place to rest. We have a doctor on board who will check you out to make sure they didn't give you some crazy disease. You will be taken care of to the best of the Federation's ability."

Looking beyond tired, the woman broke free from staring and glanced up at Rivka. "Thank you," she muttered. After laying a gentle hand on Seequa's shoulder, Rivka was nearly brought to tears by the sincerity of the woman's gratitude. She had suffered greatly at the hands of the Corranites, having been treated as no human should.

Rivka clenched her jaw and remained silent, hoping she'd be able to bring down the Corran slave trade so she would never have to deal with such a crime again.

We're on our way in. Prepare for immediate departure.

But there would be. Maybe it wouldn't be on Corran, but where there were sentient species, there would be those who exploited them. Like the Skaines.

She was even more impatient to return to her ship to

get Seequa the help she needed and find out how the others were faring in their takedowns of the cells.

The aerovan's door started to open before it touched down and Rivka helped Seequa Holmes out, keeping her hands on the young woman to make sure she didn't attack Palatius in one last act of defiance. The ship was close, a few steps, and she only had eyes for the opening hatch. Together they climbed the steps, and without a backward look, they entered and secured the ship. The crew clapped and cheered, and Tyler Toofakre helped her to a seat and started checking her vitals.

"Get her a good meal," Rivka ordered. Red held his hands up in surrender. "Meal bar?"

"On its way," Ankh said through the speakers.

Jay pulled a glass of water and handed it to the woman. "Welcome back."

Floyd stood on her back legs and shoved her head under Seequa's hand. She recoiled at the intrusion, but Floyd persisted.

"Who are you?" Seequa asked.

"Her name is Floyd," Jay offered once she realized that the young woman couldn't hear the wombat.

"Well, hello, Floyd. Are you the official greeter?" The transformation from the exhausted creature who had boarded the ship moments before to now was remarkable. Her brown eyes started to sparkle and she held out her glass.

Jay refilled it quickly.

"They didn't give us a whole lot to drink, or eat, for that matter. I always wanted to be lean and mean. Well, I've always been mean, but the lean part has avoided my crispy-fry-eating ass. Until now, that is, but I'm not sure I can recommend that diet."

Rivka snorted. "That's the attitude. It is good to have you back. Where do you want to go?"

"Back home to Elgar 7, if I can. Hopefully, I haven't lost my job. I got bills to pay." Seequa shook her head. "Ain't that some shit? I spend an eternity in that cage, and when I'm free, the first thing I think about is my damn bills."

"We made sure you didn't get evicted or fired. I expect you'll get some downtime when we get back." Rivka tried to sound reassuring. Seequa simply sighed and closed her eyes.

"Leaving the atmosphere," Chaz reported.

"It won't be long now," Lindy said as she delivered a blanket to the doc, who nodded his appreciation.

"You have a call from General Reynolds, Magistrate," Chaz reported.

"On screen." Rivka stood close to block out the others behind her.

"Good afternoon, Magistrate. I hear great things about what you're doing out there," he said casually.

Rivka nodded. "General," she greeted the nominal head of the Federation.

"I have to ask you to remain in orbit over Corran. I think I'm going to need your services sooner rather than later."

"General?"

"I think you know my guest." The camera swung to the side to show Corran's governor-general. He waved at the screen.

"Ignacio! It's nice to see you again. I admit that you have me at a disadvantage. Where are you?"

"I'm with Lance Reynolds on board my flagship in orbit over Corran."

"You're here, General?"

The image swung back until the General was centered on the screen. He raised one eyebrow at the rhetorical question.

"Keep this quiet for now," Lance said, but he lifted a pad and showed a big signature scrawled across the bottom of the screen.

Rivka collected her wits. "Welcome to the Federation, Governor-General."

"It's a bittersweet moment for my people and me, Rivka. This will be a great change for us, but one that needs to happen."

"That explains why Palatius expedited his plan for a second coup attempt. You will be safer if you make your announcement from orbit."

"I know, but I have to go back and make the announcement in Amberly," he replied sadly. It should have been a time for celebration.

"When are you going to do that?"

"Momentarily. Dock with my ship, and Lance will transfer his flag to your vessel. As soon as he's clear, we're all going to the surface to make the announcement." The governor-general raised a drink toward the screen.

"We have the coordinates, Magistrate. We'll be docking in three minutes." Chaz accelerated *Peacekeeper* toward the Corranite flagship.

"See you in a couple, Rivka." The General signed off and closed the link.

"There's going to be a slight delay in taking you home," Rivka said, still looking at the blank screen.

"Gear up?" Red asked hopefully.

"Yes," she replied. Lindy and Red pounded into the corridor to their room and started banging and bouncing off the walls as they threw on their body armor and loaded their weapons.

Jay hung her head.

"You too, Jay, Tyler."

The dentist hung his head. "This life is not for me," he said softly.

"I know, but it was worth it to show you what we do."

"I'm going too," Seequa declared. "You got any of that body armor for me?"

"Are you sure?" Rivka asked. "I can't put you in harm's way, and if I'm not mistaken, there's going to be some discontent when the Corranites are told that they aren't any better than any other Federation citizen."

"Oh, yeah. I want to see that. And that guard that hocked the king of all loogies on my face. Can I get a gun?"

"Body armor, yes. Gun? No."

The door to the bridge slid open and Ankh appeared. "Although I would prefer to remain aboard, I think that I need to be on the ground, too."

"Why is that?" Rivka wondered. He was their trump card when it came to interdicting an enemy's electronic systems.

"Because they might mistake me for Skaine, the galaxy's

slavers. With me there, they might believe the Skaines approve of the change."

"You think so?"

Ankh looked stone-faced but didn't dignify her question with an answer.

Asking all kinds of questions that you already know the answers to, she scolded herself. *I need some court time to sharpen my game. I'm losing my edge, counting on seeing people's minds. I've turned into a legal cheat.*

The ship bumped gently as it rendezvoused with the Corranite flagship.

"Airlock sealed."

Rivka hurried to the entry corridor, where the inner hatch was completing its cycle. It opened, and a distinguished gentleman stepped through. "Lance Reynolds, requesting permission to come aboard."

"Granted," Rivka replied with a smile. The two shook hands.

"I hear you're going to get a bigger ship," he told her.

"Dammit!" she replied.

"I expected something a little less disconcerting." He fixed her with a fatherly look.

"No! Not that. I'm sorry. I forgot to check in with TH after we returned with Miss Holmes." Rivka motioned for the General to follow as she took the few steps to the bridge before turning and heading into the recreation room.

"He's doing fine, still securing the Skaine vessels, but I'm happy to tell you that we've cut a major supply line. I think that was what helped us clinch the deal. The governor-general had been ready to sign, but the timing had been off. Without a new supply for the market, the traders would be more amenable to changing their line of work. It won't affect the majority of Corranites, but it *will* affect the most wealthy."

Rivka nodded as she thought through the General's explanation.

"Makes sense," she stated. "You met most of my crew on Crenellia, but that was in passing."

The General was attentive as she went from Red to Lindy to Jay, and finally to Ankh.

"You and Ted have done great things for us," the General said. "I want to give you my personal thanks for how far you've advanced us."

Lance held out his hand, but Ankh only looked at it.

"He doesn't shake hands. He's going with us because he thinks the governor-general's announcement will be better received if they think the Skaines support it."

"Brilliant!" the General declared.

Rivka pointed to the dentist and his patient. "Doctor Tyler Toofakre. He is here as my guest because we tend to get hurt a fair bit. And this is Seequa Holmes."

She stood up to greet the Federation's leader.

"Seequa. I hope that you are the last to be kidnapped and put on the auction block." He offered his hand, but she pulled him into a hug.

"I sure damn well hope so, because that sucked!"

CHAPTER TWENTY

The Skaine cruiser

The countdown timer hit zero. "Go, go, go!" Christina ordered.

The explosives carved a mech-sized hole in the rear access hatch and the hold beyond decompressed violently. As soon as the inside equalized with the outside, Team One powered through. The first warrior stepped into the hold and immediately dropped to the deck from the ship's gravity field. Gathering his feet under him, he proceeded through the cargo hold, looking for the forcefield generator. The emergency system had not activated with the breach.

The other three mech-suited warriors followed him in.

"Found it," he reported. "Give me a minute."

"Breach is stalled until we activate the emergency forcefield.

"Sorry, this isn't it."

The team leader growled his dismay. "Load a cargo pallet in front of it and seal it."

The mech's power-augmentations made short work of dumping crates from a metal pallet. He slapped it against the breach and pulled a rapid-expanding foam extinguisher off the bulkhead. Its purpose was to seal small holes in the hull.

The warrior started to spray and ran out about three-fourths of the way around. They found one more at the far end of the hold and filled the rest of the space around the pallet. The hold did not automatically fill with atmosphere.

"What's taking so damn long?" Christina demanded.

"Sealed the breach and looking for the activator to pressurize the hold."

"Hurry the fuck up!" Christina reevaluated the timing. They were at seven minutes following the start of pumping the gas in. "Teams Two and Three, secure the airlocks and pass through."

Both teams had already tapped the activation panels and were waiting to head into the lock, but only two mechs would fit inside at a time. Christina worked her way to the front of Team Two. "I'm going in first. Come on, Gefelton, we're going in. You got my six."

The outer airlock hatch rolled open and the two mechs squeezed through. They sealed themselves inside, and after they mashed the button to pressurize, a light flashed and the small space filled with air. When the light shone steady, Christina contorted her suit so it was on its side. She pressed the inner hatch button, and the barrier rolled aside.

An orange pallor hung in the inner air. Christina tried to get her bearings; the corridor angled toward the interior of the ship, not at a ninety-degree angle from the airlock. A second corridor was behind her, similarly situated at a thirty-degree angle away from the airlock. She couldn't see anyone, and she couldn't get farther into the corridor.

"Pull me back, Private."

Gefelton helped her back into the airlock and steadied her so she could stand. She turned around to face him, opened the back of her suit, and climbed out. She stepped into the corridor with her Jean Dukes Special pistol strapped to her waist. She didn't bother pulling it out. She listened carefully. The gas made her head swim.

Instead of putting her hood over her head and using the sleek shipsuit's internal air supply, she growled and started to change. Her face stretched, and her nails became nine-inch long claws. She grew in height and length of limb.

She unleashed the Pricolici within, and that creature ducked under the low ceilings of the Skaine cruiser. She stalked the corridors, sniffing and listening. Christina charged forward to find a group of unconscious Skaines manning a checkpoint. She placed a single claw across a blue throat but didn't do it. She didn't kill him. Instead, Christina took their weapons, stringing them on one of her claws until she could find a place to stash them or a better way to carry them.

The colonel continued to prowl the corridors of the ship, listening for the sounds of conscious crew. She dropped to run on four legs in the jerky style of one whose back legs are longer than their front. Christina stayed low as she ran through the corridors, and everywhere she looked, the crew was out cold.

She opened door after door, ducking and dodging so

she wasn't outlined in case a Skaine with a weapon was hiding within.

But none of them were. Terry and Char had assaulted the cutter before the gas had time to take effect.

The Pricolici relaxed and strolled through the last hatch leading to the bridge.

The plasma burst hit her mid-chest and threw her back into the corridor to slam into the far wall. She slid down it and crumpled to the floor as the bridge access closed.

Amberly on Corran

Peacekeeper followed the flagship into the upper atmosphere through the flames of re-entry, and descended toward the planet, slowing before arriving at the outer limits of the capital city. The larger ship took a leisurely route over Amberly where the citizens could see it.

The governor-general sought to make the biggest impression as part of his grand announcement.

Politics. It was a different animal.

General Reynolds sat on one of the chairs at the table, even though Rivka offered him the recliner. She joined him at the table and turned over the comfortable seat to Jay and Floyd. Lindy and Red leaned against the kitchen counter in full combat gear. Tyler continued to minister to Seequa, but after ingesting both food and water, she was remarkably improved.

"Why don't you use the bridge?" General Reynolds asked. Red and Lindy chuckled as they waited for Rivka's revelation.

The Magistrate hesitated a long time before answering,

but the General waited. He was the father of a daughter, so he knew that sometimes there was no rushing an answer.

She finally blurted, "Ankh needed it more than I did." She didn't add the part where she'd reassigned his laboratory.

"I can see that. If he was on my team, I'd give him whatever he wants too. Is that all you had to promise him?"

"Well…yes." Rivka was surprised by the question.

"Hell! You won that arbitration. Well done, Magistrate!"

"I don't feel like I won." She swept her arm to take in the rec room.

"Trust me, you won." The General looked at the team. "When we hit the ground, we back up the governor-general. Even though Corran is now a member of the Federation, there is a phase-in, phase-out period. Slavery will be illegal in due course. No new sales will be allowed, but old contracts are still in effect. Instead of new sales, salaries and benefits will be negotiated with the labor force, and each worker given an advocate. Sorry, I don't need to get into those details. This is Ignacio's show. We'll follow his lead. I'll say some kind words about how we value our new friends from Corran and so on.

"I'm proud to say that I've made this speech dozens of times. I think the Federation is stronger because of our new members. Corran will be the same. Over time, they'll be great, and their participation will be important to give us a more rounded group, diverse in all aspects of ideas and history. We are stronger together."

"I've told my team the same thing, General. Thanks for letting us tag along."

The General started to laugh. "We'll see if Ankh can

convince them that the Skaines support Corran's move to the Federation. It's doubtful that he can sell it, but worth a shot. We have to take any chance to stop a shooting war." The General leaned forward to get close to Rivka. "You said that there was going to be a second coup attempt. The governor-general is counting on it. When the shooting starts, I need your team to secure the governor-general while the loyal troops reestablish control."

"What if the loyal troops don't win?"

"Then we'll give them a little nudge so they do."

"There are only six of us, General."

"Like I said, a *little* nudge."

Rivka looked skeptical. The General smiled back, appearing unconcerned.

She had a difficult time reconciling the man before her with the leader of the Federation. Leader. Of the Federation. Then it dawned on her.

"You have an ace up your sleeve."

"IF you ain't cheating, you ain't trying," Lance Reynolds admitted. "Only a few rich Corranites will be put out, but they earned their money at the expense of other people's lives, so screw them. Nothing gives me greater pleasure than seeing Justice delivered."

"Me too, General." Rivka nodded as she replied. When she turned, she found the rest of the team nodding in agreement.

Lance stood and headed for the hatch. "Looks like we're almost there."

Red hurried to get in front. "Sorry, General. I always go out first."

"Because we need the sun blocked?" Lance quipped. Lindy snickered as she passed.

"And me. We need to make sure it's safe for the Magistrate. It's what we do," Lindy explained.

"I'll stay close to her, then." The General winked at Rivka.

"My daughter always had people watching out for her, but she watched out for them, too."

"It's what good leaders do." Rivka studied the father of the Queen. She could feel the aura he radiated. She didn't understand how he was so much bigger than life, but real as well. She had dedicated her life to following and supporting him.

Now that she'd had the opportunity to spend some time with the man, her career path was confirmed. She was doing the right thing as a Federation Magistrate.

For the greater good of the galaxy. Even if they did shoot at her more often than she liked.

"What?" General Reynolds asked, looking at her glistening eyes. He reached over to her face and with a gentle finger, brushed the tear away that fell.

He stopped as the ship settled and Red hesitated, waiting for the General to stop speaking before he opened the hatch.

"Let me share my favorite poem from Robert Frost.

> *"Two roads diverged in a yellow wood,*
> *And sorry I could not travel both*
> *And be one traveler, long I stood*
> *And looked down one as far as I could*
> *To where it bent in the undergrowth;*

Then took the other, as just as fair,
And having perhaps the better claim,
Because it was grassy and wanted wear;
Though as for that the passing there
Had worn them really about the same,

And both that morning equally lay
In leaves no step had trodden black.
Oh, I kept the first for another day!
Yet knowing how way leads on to way,
I doubted if I should ever come back.

I shall be telling this with a sigh
Somewhere ages and ages hence:
Two roads diverged in a wood, and I—
I took the one less travelled by,
And that has made all the difference."

"Beautiful," Rivka replied not having heard it before.

"It's how I've lived my life. It's how my daughter has lived hers. It has made for a better life for both of us. I think you are on the path trod lightly, leaving your tracks for others to follow you." The General looked at the bulkhead and realized that they were parked. "Shall we?"

Red opened the airlock before anyone else became too emotional, and Lindy smirked at her chosen partner's discomfort. His idea of being emotional was getting angry after being kneed in the groin.

The sunny day belied the dark cloud hanging over them. The governor-general was already glad-handing his way toward a stage that had been set up at the edge of the capital city's central park. His flagship hovered overhead, and the shuttle he'd used to land was parked in front of Rivka's corvette. Their two ships took up all the available landing space.

Rich Corranites who flew in for the live event would have to get dropped off. There was no executive parking. Rivka thought it would make her a target. The Federation's Magistrate Corps logo was emblazoned on the side. There was no doubt who they represented.

If the coup attempt was made, she wondered if her ship would be targeted.

Red and Lindy walked up front, with Rivka and General Reynolds behind them. Ankh, Jay, Seequa, and Tyler followed. Rivka glanced back and saw Floyd bouncing happily along.

If there's any shooting, you protect Floyd, Rivka told Jay, not pleased that the wombat had left the ship. But if they attacked the ship, she'd be inside, alone and afraid. Maybe it was best that she stay with them.

Hamlet was on his own. He never left the ship.

If anyone attacks my ship, they need to be sanctioned with extreme prejudice, she said.

I'm good with that, Red replied.

Consider it done, Magistrate, Lindy added. She carried her railgun in a way that suggested she'd been born with one in her hands. It seemed like a natural extension of her body as she walked. Red was the same: comfortable but ready to engage an enemy.

They both walked with a confident swagger, eyes never resting on one thing for long while they classified each person or object as a threat or non-threat.

Rivka and General Reynolds only had eyes for the governor-general. He waved to the crowd, who gave him a half-hearted wave in return, but he angled toward the humans.

When the two groups merged, the governor-general's personal escort swarmed around Rivka and her team. Red and Lindy stood back to back in order to keep eyes on them all.

I find it interesting that we're given the closest access to their boss, Lindy offered.

Maybe that's part of the deal since General Reynolds is here, Rivka replied to her team.

He is *more important.*

It's good that they agree. Would you look at that? Rivka asked, tipping her head toward the stage.

Palatius Lore, Red confirmed.

CHAPTER TWENTY-ONE

Skaine cruiser

"What is that thing?" the muffled voice of the ship's commander came through an air filtering mask. Four Skaines slunk out from behind their stations on the bridge, plasma rifles aimed at Christina's prone body. She remained in Pricolici form, and the steady rise and fall of her chest told them she was still alive.

And thanks to her nanocytes, she was getting better with each passing second.

But could she survive four more point-blank plasma bursts?

"I've never seen anything like it," another stated.

"It'll fetch a bulk of credits. Can we get the engines back online?" the commander asked. He stepped into the corridor and nudged the Pricolici with the barrel of his rifle. "I thought that was a human ship out there..."

A hand blaster barked, and the Skaine's head exploded in a mist of blue and gore. A second round took the next Skaine in the chest. The last two ducked onto the bridge as

Christina's eyes opened. She blinked to get her bearings and understand what was going on.

The Skaines fired haphazardly into the corridor to suppress the incoming shots. They discharged their plasma rifles again, one after the other. Whoever had joined the battle had sought cover, the Pricolici reasoned, since the enemy was still firing.

She bared her fangs and rolled to her stomach, then bunched her back legs beneath her, stifling a growl as the fire surged through her veins. The plasma rifle barrels appeared again and fired. Christina launched herself past the coming, grabbing both barrels and ripping them away from the startled Skaines.

While the weapons went sailing across the bridge, the Pricolici slashed back.

The last expressions on their faces morphed from surprise to shock. She stood over the bodies and roared her victory before settling on her haunches and changing back into human form. Her shipsuit had been modified to account for the changes, but the plasma blast had destroyed the front of the suit. When it contracted, her chest remained exposed. She grunted at it before ripping the jacket from a Skaine who had been too slow getting his mask on and draping it over herself.

A warrior appeared behind her.

"Are you all right, ma'am?"

"I am. Thanks for the save, Private. Did you come through the airlock?"

"Yes, but it's now blocked. There's only room for one mech suit in there."

Christina nodded and switched to the internal comm.

Ship is clear. Ditch your mechs outside and get in here, people. Start securing these prisoners before they wake up. Smedley, get into their systems and determine if there's anything we want before we decide if we're going to keep it or scuttle it. And where in the hell is Team One?

Sorry, ma'am. We're still in the hold.

And now you've welded yourselves in and can't pressurize or get out?

That doesn't sound like the write-up I wanted to see on my medal, the team leader replied.

Hurry up over there. We have some business to take care of, Terry Henry interjected.

Amberly on Corran

The governor-general worked his way to the stage, stopping to greet each of the dour dignitaries. He talked animatedly in a most un-Corranite way. General Reynolds and Rivka remained nearby, nodding courteously but not engaging the Corranites. Rivka pulled Ankh to her, keeping him close. The locals were far more interested in him than they were in the humans or their gregarious leader.

Never take a politician for a fool. They didn't get where they are because they don't understand. They take in massive amounts of information and reduce that to an action that they can take that will appeal to the majority of the people. The governor-general knew that he had to tolerate the others on the stage, but he also had to placate those in the audience. Balancing the two was a politician's perpetual challenge.

He was polite to the humans but became animated once again when he brought the Crenellian to the fore. Ankh strolled along, small hands clasped behind his back as he tried to look attentive.

Jay, Tyler, and Seequa didn't climb onto the stage. They remained off to the side, next to the stairs. The former captive's nostrils flared as she glared at the Corranites on stage.

I'm not sure if we should be more wary of the people on the stage or those in the audience, Red complained. *Request permission to take a position behind dignitary row. Lindy will remain next to the governor-general and the Magistrate.*

Sounds like a good plan, Rivka replied, looking back and forth between the two groups. She caught Palatius Lore staring at her with the look of a serial killer. She'd seen it before, and stared back. She tipped her chin to him and mouthed the words, "You die first."

Lore looked around as Red moved behind the row of dignitaries to stand behind him. When the governor-general's aide tried to move, Red grabbed his shoulder and held him in place.

Ignacio Mar ended his glad-handing and took his position behind the lectern. He held up his arms in the universal sign of victory, turning back and forth so everyone could see his exuberance.

"What a great day to be alive!" he started.

Rivka steeled herself not to react. She hoped, knowing that hope was a lousy plan, that when the day ended, those in attendance would still be alive. She expected that not all of them would see the sunset.

"I asked for this gathering to announce a new and

greater direction for the people of Corran. Greater prof-
itability, an improved standard of living, and travel to
exotic places that were previously closed to us. How do we
get there? That's the question I'm going to answer shortly.
But first, I'd like our Skaine representative to say a few
words.

Here we go, Rivka thought, clapping politely as Ankh
stepped up a staircase that a stagehand had moved into
place so the crowd could see him.

"The Skaines have been providing capital for resale, but
we have now ceased that operation." He made to get down,
but the governor-general wrapped a protective arm
around him and waved to the silent crowd.

Rivka's lip twitched into a smile. Ankh hadn't lied.

"As you know, the Skaines provide less than half of
those we route through our marketplace, but they aren't
the only ones who have shut down operations. Too many
have been driven out of business, which has forced us to
rethink our role in an expanding galaxy. No one wants to
lose what they have, but lose it you will, regardless of how.
If we let go and reach forward, we will progress as a
people.

"Hang on to what will inexorably be left behind, and
you will be pulled into the abyss of irrelevance. Join me in
moving forward. Corran will blossom like a Langiss Rainbow. It's right there, and all we have to do is grab it."

Corranites were not prone to raucous celebration, but
the words of support and encouragement were bold,
filling the field with sound. No one clapped. It wasn't
their way.

Be ready, Rivka said, more to herself than the others.

Floyd wriggled out of Jay's arms and landed on the stage with a thump that relayed through the microphone.

The governor-general finally let go of Ankh, and the Crenellian hurried down the stairs. Floyd almost knocked him over in her joy at seeing him.

"And now," the Ignacio continued, giving the stagehand space to remove the small staircase. "The leader of the Etheric Federation, General Lance Reynolds."

The General moved forward, and Rivka grabbed the wombat and picked her up.

Magistrate? Red asked, knowing that she couldn't fight while carrying Floyd. Tension filled the stage from those with the most to lose. *These fuckers are getting antsy.*

She ignored him and tried to look like she wasn't hurrying to get rid of the wombat. She cooed in Floyd's ear and headed for the stairs.

"Good afternoon, esteemed citizens of Corran. I'll keep this short because no one likes to stand around and listen to politicians. As of nine Yoll-standard time this morning, Corran is our newest member in what is a robust and growing alliance between civilizations. We believe that the whole is greater than the sum of our parts. We are better together. Welcome to the Federation."

Palatius ducked from under Red's hand and started to bolt forward. With a ninja-like maneuver, the big man kicked Lore's chair into his legs. The Corranite tripped and went down, and Red jumped to straddle him and drove a heavy fist into the back of his head. Lore's face slammed into the stage. Red stepped back where he could see the others on the platform. Most of the dignitaries were standing.

Red covered them with his railgun, but none challenged the bodyguard's threat. *Behind me?* he asked.

You're clear, Lindy replied. She turned back to the audience, keeping the business end of her weapon pointed skyward. They appeared disconnected from the machinations on stage.

The governor-general glanced behind him, shrugging at the prone form of his former aide. Ignacio stepped to the microphone and spoke again.

"I will tell you about opportunity and a shining light ahead of us, but there will be a change to the way Corran conducts itself. Trading in the lives of sentient species is a significant part of our history, but has grown less and less over the years. It now accounts for less than twenty percent of our economy, and of that, less than five percent is from forced sales. Selling labor against their will is now a crime. By the end of the day, my office will transmit the required contractual provisions. Compliance with their inclusion is mandatory."

Rivka finally nuzzled the wombat sufficiently that Floyd let go. Jay took her back and reported over the internal comm, *Incoming.*

A group of armed security headed toward the stage, where the governor-general was waving at them and pointing.

Who do I shoot? Red asked.

No one, Rivka replied. *I think this is the counter-coup. He should have told us.*

The security team arrived on stage and started manhandling the dignitaries, pushing them into the middle of the stage where there was more room. As one, the rich and powerful dropped to the floor and the guards started firing.

The Royal City of Khn'Chik on Yoll

The High Chancellor was reading the latest sheaf of reports on his datapad as he waited for the Parmecium to come to. He had removed the top on the travel container and poured Beauregard into a bowl on the interrogation table. His device remained at hand if she needed to be neutralized. The box that translated her thoughts into human speech sat nearby.

Grainger leaned against the wall, lost in his own thoughts.

The liquid started to undulate, slowly at first, but then formed into a small shape that flowed from the bowl and started to expand. She assumed a humanoid shape and sat on her side of the table. Wyatt finished what he was reading and casually turned off his pad. He leaned back and took a deep breath but didn't speak.

"Where?" the Parmecium asked in her digitally-generated female voice.

"Interrogation room, Khn'Chik detention center," Wyatt answered.

"Why?"

"Tell us where to find Vaidyn."

"No."

"Yes," Wyatt countered with equal indifference.

"Okay," Malagor Beauregard replied.

"What?" Grainger blurted. "It never works that way!"

The High Chancellor addressed the Magistrate's surprise with an icy gaze. Grainger winced.

"A Corranite."

"That is something we didn't know, and it narrows it down. Which one?" Wyatt waited, but the Parmecium didn't expound. "Answer that last question and I will open the door so you can walk out of here free and clear, with one caution. Don't attempt to return to the slave trade. Should you be unable to control yourself, I will have you burned in the fire pits."

"Palatius Lore."

Bad Company Destroyer *War Axe*

"We need to go!" TH almost yelled through the comm system. The hangar was buzzing with activity as the Skaine bodies were removed from the cutter. Technicians from the War Axe crew were swarming aboard to assess the ship and start making repairs.

"The damn airlocks are too small, and my people are scattered across half the ship rounding up groggy blueheads. I still have a team trapped in the hold, but we're making progress there, too. Leave us here. We'll figure it out, but don't forget where we parked!"

"Drop a resupply food can and punch it!" Terry shouted over his shoulder. Two warriors bolted for the aft storage area, where canisters were filled based on a variety of mission basics. The food canister contained food and water for a full platoon for a month. With only twelve warriors on the Skaine cruiser, they'd be well taken care of. TH expected the War Axe would be back in a matter of days. Twelve warriors weren't enough to guard the hundred devious bastards they had in custody.

The canister rolled by, with the two volunteers hustling it along. Four others joined them as they ran it to the open door and pushed it into the void of space. It floated toward the Skaine ship.

"You might want to get someone to grab that thing before it smashes into you or skips past and disappears. And by all that's holy, be careful," Terry told Christina before switching channels. "Micky, Gate us out of here."

The *War Axe* shifted orientation to face away from the Skaine ship. The Gate formed, and the ship accelerated into it.

Amberly on Corran

Lindy tackled the General, powering forward to take down the governor-general too. She rolled to the side to shield them with her body.

"Fuck, no!" Red roared, clicking his railgun to full auto as he shredded the Corranite ranks. Someone fired from behind him, hitting his legs repeatedly with heavy slugs. He staggered, and his barrel tipped toward the distinguished guests. He let off the trigger as a barrage of incoming fire slammed into his body. He stumbled and went down.

Rivka dove on top of the two men, having no plan beyond that. She knew she had to do something, and started to dig in her pocket for Reaper. She was ready to unleash its power, if only she could find her targets.

Lindy started firing from her position, but she couldn't swing the barrel to take in all the targets. After Red went down, rounds started to impact Lindy. She grunted from the pain and stopped firing when a slug tore through her fingers.

The insurrectionists stopped firing as Jay ran by the group huddled behind the stage, ripping the weapons from their hands. She dumped the slug throwers on the stage and leaned over to check on Red. A new round of fire started from the far side of the stage, closer to the audience.

"Get down!" Rivka yelled as a slug hit Jay in the chest and sent her spinning head over heels and off the stage.

The General was trying to rise, growling and grunting to get up without throwing people off. Rivka jumped to her feet and ran straight at the four Corranites who had been hiding in plain sight in the front row. They adjusted fire, but Rivka was already airborne, waving Reaper clicked to the highest setting.

The shooters wilted like flowers before a flame. The last round fired creased the side of her face, upsetting her balance so she landed flat on her side, rolling to a stop before she collected her wits enough to stand. She backed up to the stage and looked for a new enemy.

Tyler bolted across the stage, jumping over Red and vaulting off the stage to land next to Jay. He rolled her over to get a better look at her injuries. Seequa Holmes appeared on stage, ripping a slug thrower from one of the dead guards and stalking forward, looking for any Corranite to challenge her.

Palatius started to crawl toward the side, and she shot him in the leg. He yowled, trying to crawl faster but dragging his injured leg behind him. Seequa ran two steps, reared back, and swung her weapon aiming at the fibrous skin that covered his head. She hit him with everything left of her strength and delivered an injury from which he would not recover.

Seeing the damage, Seequa Holmes stumbled to her knees and puked over the edge of the stage.

"We need to get back to the ship," Tyler said urgently in the silence of the aftermath.

General Reynolds pulled the governor-general upright, and they surveyed the area. Chaos ensued from the audience, who trampled each other trying to get away from the cacophony of battle. Ankh appeared from where he'd hidden inside the heavy cabinet of the lectern.

Floyd cried into everyone's minds.

The General looked at Lindy, who pointed at Red. Reynolds hurried to him and checked for a pulse, and immediately lifted the big man into his arms. The concern on his face drove Lindy to climb to her feet despite the blood streaming from a dozen wounds on her body.

Rivka jumped onto the stage to assess the damage, but the blood flowing down her head ran into her eye. She rubbed it away, unconcerned with her own health. Half her crew was being carried by the other half.

A massive fireball appeared in the sky.

"Back to the ship!" Rivka ordered.

"Wait!" the General ordered. "These two need a Pod-doc, and they need it right goddamn now."

"We can Gate out from within the atmosphere," Rivka declared.

"We can't," Ankh clarified.

"Any Pod-docs on Corran?" she asked the governor-general.

"No. That's forbidden technology for non-members," he explained, but she had stopped listening after the word 'no.' The Magistrate pulled Lindy close so she could lean on her as they headed for the stairs.

CHAPTER TWENTY-TWO

The fireball coalesced into a great hulking warship streaking toward them far too quickly. It came to an abrupt stop and settled toward the chairs and tents of the audience area. The remainder of the crowd dashed out of its way. The *War Axe* landed, crushing whatever was beneath it.

The forcefield protecting the hangar bay shimmered and then went out as people dressed in combat uniforms appeared, jumped to the ground and started forming a defensive perimeter.

The dentist ran past Rivka with Jay in his arms and the wombat on his heels. The General caught up to him despite carrying the huge bodyguard. Rivka and Lindy did the three-legged shuffle, falling behind with each step. Ankh was running and yelling that he needed to be there. Seequa Holmes and the governor-general ran up, each grabbing an arm to carry the Crenellian to the destroyer.

Terry and Char ran down the short ramp to intercept the group and guide them to sickbay. Terry took Ankh in hand and yelled that he'd meet them upstairs. While the others went for the elevator, TH accelerated to a speed that strained even his abilities. He hit the doorway off the hangar bay and vaulted nearly a flight of steps in a single leap. He bounced off the bulkhead before turning and repeating the feat. Reaching the level where medical was located, he ran, sliding to a stop to drop Ankh off well before the others arrived.

Ankh hurried inside, chased away the technician, and brought up the holoscreens, instantly engaging with Erasmus and his considerable intellect to ensure that the Magistrate's crew was taken care of.

Tyler arrived first with Jay, depositing her into the Pod-doc. The cover closed.

The dentist stood and looked at it. "What now?"

"We wait," Terry told him.

"How long?" General Reynolds asked.

"Don't know, but she was alive when she went in, so she'll be fine when she comes out."

"How long?" General Reynolds repeated.

Terry gritted his teeth in frustration. Ankh was deep within the holographic interface and wasn't up for answering questions.

Red bled heavily from too many wounds. His nanocytes couldn't keep up.

"Don't let him die," Lindy pleaded from the doorway.

The click of a dog's nails on the deck plating echoed down the corridor as Dokken ran toward them. He slid into Rivka, nearly knocking her down. Floyd whined from somewhere in the ship. She hadn't made it to Medical yet.

Relax, little girl. We're doing all we can, TH told her.

"Let her through!" Char yelled.

Cordelia Dawn appeared in the crush of people outside the sickbay. "Put him down," she ordered the General, who complied without hesitation.

She knelt next to Red and looked him over quickly before putting one hand on a wound in his neck and the other on his shoulder. She closed her glowing blue eyes and the same glow appeared beneath her hands, increasing in intensity with each passing second. She pressed her eyes closed, furrowing her brow with the effort.

Red's breathing slowed, until with a single exhale, he stopped.

Lindy gasped and started to cry. The governor-general and Seequa Holmes leaned against each other as they hung their heads.

"Shhh," Charumati said, taking the woman by the arm and smiling reassuringly.

With a heave, Red arched his back, sucked in a huge lungful of air, and opened his eyes. His breathing was initially rapid and shallow, but it started to slow and deepen. His eyes fluttered open.

Cory's arms sagged and the blue glow faded. She sat heavily and almost fell over. Terry lifted her and held her.

"That mission sucked," Red grumbled.

"Fine," Rivka conceded. "We'll call that one a mission, but the rest are cases. Don't make me fight you on that."

"Welcome to the *War Axe*, General Reynolds, Governor-General Mar." Micky beamed at his guests.

"I appreciate the timeliness of your arrival, Skipper," the General said, using the nickname Terry Henry had given Micky. "I always appreciate fireworks when someone joins the Federation, but usually we aren't on the receiving end of the exploding stuff."

"I'd like to say that my people have things under control, but there's still a little strife at the central market. It appears that some of those being traded held a grudge against the guards. A few were torn apart, so the newly freed celebrated by getting themselves arrested for murder."

"I hope we can talk about that before anyone goes to prison," the General warned.

Rivka and TH entered the conference room with a few others on their heels. "There's an awful lot of revision that needs to happen with your legal system, Ignacio. The Federation supports planets in how they govern themselves, but I have some personal issues with the way your laws are written." Rivka had been on the wrong end of those laws, and if they remained as they were, former slaves would get arrested and become slaves once again.

That was the General's point in avoiding quick sentencing.

"I am open to a complete rewrite. I hope that you will be able to stay and provide some oversight of the process." The governor-general looked contrite and sincere.

"I will not be able to, but I can make a few recommendations. My class from law school was filled with sharp minds who would rise to this challenge. I'll make some calls."

Reynolds nodded at Rivka in appreciation of her offer.

Jay appeared, carrying Floyd. The group parted and offered her a seat. She didn't argue. "I thought the Pod-doc was supposed to rejuvenate me, but I feel tired."

Floyd cheered with a hearty, *Wheeee!*

TH scratched behind her ears. "I miss you, Floyd," he said.

Miss you, too. You're still mine, she replied happily.

Terry's smile slowly faded. "Don't tell me you pooped outside our door."

Char shook her head.

It's how I tell everyone how much I love them.

Terry had no comeback.

"That's okay, little girl," Terry conceded reluctantly.

"Where's that dentist?" General Reynolds asked.

Rivka moved slowly out of the General's line of sight.

"Here, General!" Tyler called from the corridor outside.

The two men approached each other for a hearty hand-shake. "I appreciate what you did to help the victims and the crew."

"My pleasure, General, but don't ask me to go out there again. That is not my cup of go-juice."

"I don't blame you. Rivka runs on rocket fuel and Moonstokle pie."

"Yes!" Terry pumped his fist. "Did you get that, Smed-ley? Tell me you got that. Gin up an ad to flood Keeg Station. The leader of the Etheric Federation says the Magistrate runs on rocket fuel and Moonstokle pie, avail-able from TH's All Guns Blazing!"

"Aren't you taking liberties, Colonel?" Reynolds asked.

"Absolutely! Most people don't eat that crap, but they won't know they need it until we tell them." TH grinned.

"I better get back," the governor-general interrupted. "I don't want the masses to think I've abandoned them. "Miss Holmes, shall we?"

"You're going to stay on Corran?" Rivka wondered.

"The interim Ambassador," the General replied before Seequa could. "I think if anyone can keep the focus on dismantling the slave trade, it will be her."

"You got that right, Lance," Seequa replied, giving the General a fist-bump.

"I better get going as well," the General told them. He looked at Micky. "Just one thing: I need a ride to orbit."

"Take my ship, General," Rivka offered.

"I think your ship is on the hangar deck of the *War Axe*," he replied. "I'll take your old ride, but you can transfer your stuff first. My people won't be here for a few hours. In the interim, if I can get a private space with a comm link, I have some work to do. Never a dull moment in the Etheric Federation."

"You can have this space, General." The two shook hands, and Micky shooed everyone out.

"Behold, Magistrate! Your chariot," Terry said proudly, sweeping an arm wide to take in the entirety of the cutter.

"What the hell happened to my new ship?" Rivka asked.

"You didn't think the Skaines were just going to give it to us, did you?"

"I think we need a better definition of 'new,'" Red grumbled, leaning against the doorframe with Lindy hugging him tightly.

The group headed inside the ship. Rivka wore a look of shock.

"Grenades?" Red asked.

"An unfortunately large number of them," TH admitted. "But after a fresh coat of paint, no one will know the difference."

"I should have known!" Ankh looked up at the colonel. "The destroyer of all things."

"Hey, little buddy!" Terry said in a friendly voice. "If your evil twins would have played nice..."

"We need a real engineer," Chaz interrupted over the ship's comm system.

"Oh, good. You're on board. What's the damage?" Rivka asked.

"Besides the affront to my dignity? There are significant issues with key systems. Additionally, the power source, Gate drive, and transmitters have not yet been installed. It'll be a week of one-hundred-percent effort to get this thing ready to fly."

"Great!" Rivka replied to everyone's surprise. "I could use some downtime."

"You want me to work in this bucket?" Lieutenant Clodagh Shortall asked, looking as shocked at Rivka had.

"Yes," Ankh said.

"Okay, but on one condition. You have to rescue my boyfriend. Someone abandoned him in interstellar space."

"The destroyer of all things..." Ankh mumbled.

"I'm telling you—a fresh coat of paint, maybe some pictures. You'll grow to love it."

"Will we ever get the smell out?" Jay asked, walking

slowly through the cutters' narrow corridors. "Where's Hamlet?"

"On that..." Rivka started.

"You didn't leave him on *Peacekeeper*, did you?" Jay demanded.

"No. He left of his own accord. Seems he stowed away. Again." Rivka took out her datapad and tapped a few buttons. She held it up for the others to see. Hamlet was curled up in a small case of clothes.

General Reynolds' clothes.

The End

Judge, Jury, & Executioner, Book 5

If you like this book, please leave a review. This is a new series, so the only way I can decide whether to commit more time to it is by getting feedback from you, the readers. Your opinion matters to me. Continue or not? I have only so much time to craft new stories. Help me invest that time wisely. Plus, reviews buoy my spirits and stoke the fires of creativity.

Don't stop now! Keep turning the pages as Craig & Michael talk about their thoughts on this book and the overall project called the Age of Expansion.

Your new favorite legal eagle will return!

AUTHOR NOTES - CRAIG MARTELLE

WRITTEN FEBRUARY 1, 2019

You are still reading! Thank you for staying on board until now. It doesn't get much better than that.

The names! So many names in this volume. I browse the internet to come up with some, and others I name after people in my life.

Amberly is named on behalf of Amberlina Alvezios, daughter of my good friend Stephen Lee. She and her family are settling into life with their new baby Amelia. Congratulations! Amberly is the jewel of Corran.

The alien from Rawfield – that's for Rita A. Whinfield (RAW field). Rita is a stalwart fan who is always ready with kind words about my stories. She deserves her own shout out.

I named Markmal's chief of operations "Candi Matz," a name provided by Chrisa Changala. I work closely with the fans who follow me on the Kurtherian Gambit Fans and Authors Facebook group. That's where I'll ask for names or planets or aliens, or just about anything. And Tracie Martin provided Fenek Eudoxius for the planet where they were headed. I asked for a variety of names—a man, a woman, a male, a female, a raving lunatic, and a butthole. You never know when a butthole is going to pop out of nowhere and need an appropriate designation. So there we have it.

Ch'ta'ka came from Kathleen Snowberger as an alien name in my butthole-name-question. My compliments to the great Kurtherian Gambit readers for coming up with names for me.

Curt Spa provided the names of his grandchildren—so exotic. Zaiden, Klavin, and Vaidyn. They all deserve to be in a bestselling science fiction story. Thanks, Curt, for chiming in.

I've quoted Robert Frost's poem, *The Road Not Taken* in its entirety, which is legal. The poem is in the public domain for anyone to use. It is a beautiful example of flow and impact. It is my favorite poem, and I thought it appropriate for that moment in the story.

Peace, fellow humans.

Please join my Newsletter (www.craigmartelle.com – please, please, please sign up!), or you can follow me on Facebook since you'll get the same opportunity to pick up the books for only 99 cents on that first day they are published.

If you liked this story, you might like some of my

other books. You can join my mailing list by dropping by my website **www.craigmartelle.com** or if you have any comments, shoot me a note at craig@craigmartelle.com. I am always happy to hear from people who've read my work. I try to answer every email I receive.

If you liked the story, please write a short review for me on Amazon. I greatly appreciate any kind words, even one or two sentences go a long way. The number of reviews an ebook receives greatly improves how well an ebook does on Amazon.

Amazon – www.amazon.com/author/craigmartelle

BookBub – https://www.bookbub.com/authors/craig-martelle

Facebook – www.facebook.com/authorcraigmartelle

My web page – www.craigmartelle.com

That's it—break's over, back to writing the next book. Peace, fellow humans.

BOOKS BY CRAIG MARTELLE

Craig Martelle's other books (listed by series)

For a complete list of books from Craig, please see
www.craigmartelle.com<u>**Craig Martelle's other books (listed by series)**</u>

Terry Henry Walton Chronicles (co-written with Michael Anderle) – a post-apocalyptic paranormal adventure

Gateway to the Universe (co-written with Justin Sloan & Michael Anderle) – this book transitions the characters from the Terry Henry Walton Chronicles to The Bad Company

The Bad Company (co-written with Michael Anderle) – a military science fiction space opera

End Times Alaska (also available in audio) – a Permuted Press publication – a post-apocalyptic survivalist adventure

The Free Trader – a Young Adult Science Fiction Action Adventure

Cygnus Space Opera – A Young Adult Space Opera (set in the Free Trader universe)

Darklanding (co-written with Scott Moon) – a Space Western

Judge, Jury, & Executioner – a space opera adventure legal thriller

Rick Banik – Spy & Terrorism Action Adventure

Become a Successful Indie Author – a non-fiction work

Metamorphosis Alpha – stories from the world's first science fiction RPG

The Expanding Universe – science fiction anthologies

Shadow Vanguard – a Tom Dublin series

Enemy of my Enemy (co-written with Tim Marquitz) – A galactic alien military space opera

Superdreadnought (co-written with Tim Marquitz) – an AI military space opera

Metal Legion (co-written with Caleb Wachter) – a galactic military sci-fi with mechs

End Days (co-written with E.E. Isherwood) – a post-apocalyptic adventure

Mystically Engineered (co-written with Valerie Emerson) – dragons in space

Monster Case Files (co-written with Kathryn Hearst) – a young-adult cozy mystery series

BOOKS BY MICHAEL ANDERLE

For a complete list of books by Michael Anderle, please visit:

www.lmbpn.com/ma-books/

All LMBPN Audiobooks are Available at Audible.com and iTunes

To see all LMBPN audiobooks, including those written by
Michael Anderle please visit:

www.lmbpn.com/audible